MAGIC

T0349256

MAGIC

SARAH PINBOROUGH

First published in Great Britain in 2024 by Gollancz
an imprint of The Orion Publishing Group Ltd
Carmelite House, 50 Victoria Embankment
London EC4Y 0DZ

An Hachette UK Company

The authorised representative in the EEA is Hachette Ireland,
8 Castlecourt Centre, Dublin 15, D15 XTP3, Ireland (email: info@hbgi.ie)

5 7 9 10 8 6 4

A CIP catalogue record for this book is
available from the British Library.

ISBN (Paperback) 978 1 399 62348 3
ISBN (eBook) 978 1 399 62349 0
ISBN (Audio) 978 1 399 62350 6

Typeset by Input Data Services Ltd, Bridgwater, Somerset

Printed in Great Britain by Clays Ltd, Elcograf S.p.A

MIX
Paper | Supporting
responsible forestry
FSC
www.fsc.org FSC® C104740

www.gollancz.co.uk

For Gillian, of course, who else?
We've been on such a journey together
and these fairy tales will always feel like
they're 'ours' not mine.
Thank you for everything.

One

It was the early hours of the morning and even the moon slept, hidden behind thick clouds, knitting a better blanket of darkness around Aladdin than any invisibility spell. He carefully pulled himself up the rope he'd hooked over the side of the wealthy boat, his slim, small body barely a shadow against the mahogany wood.

The Kingdom of the Eastern Seas was a busy trading hub filled with life, traders coming equally from the frozen western climes of the aptly named Barbaric Lands and from the mainland, as people chose coastal travel rather than cutting across other kingdoms and through forests that so often had a mind of their own. There was always a wait for a space in the busy harbour of Port Sinbad, and this vessel from the Meridien

Isles was no exception. Tonight, that was serving him well.

It was a hot night and the sea had been mercifully calm for his swim, but he was still glad to be free of the water and the creatures which lived in it as he dropped quietly over the side and crouched, his blade in his hand. He needn't have feared discovery, for the polished deck was empty, save for one dour guard, sitting under a hanging glass lamp, snoring quietly with an empty wine jug by his side.

Aladdin crept closer, brown eyes thoughtful as the guard let out a satisfied grunt that suggested deep dreams of ale houses and the famous brothels of Sinbad that waited for him on dry land. The man was in no danger of waking. If Aladdin moved fast he could be off the boat again in less than half an hour, which, given how much wine the guard – who was no youth – had drunk, was plenty of time.

Still, Aladdin didn't move, instead studying the dark hairs that sprouted from the guard's wine-reddened and pock-marked nose. The fingers linked across the heavy belly were fat as a king's venison sausages. Both the nose hair and the fingers reminded Aladdin of his father, the spice merchant, and how he would sleep in the old wooden chair by the small fire after a hard day lugging sacks of brightly coloured powders, sugared almonds and other delicacies onto his cart to sell at the covered markets, and then bring home again to their small house, eat the dinner prepared by his wife, and sleep and start again the next day.

His father had been proud of his work even though it had never provided them with more than an honest living. His spices were of the highest quality and he could have sold them for more to the cooks at every castle in the Nine Kingdoms, but he preferred to work in the loud and lively markets where ordinary people bought and sold their wares.

To be a spice seller was a family tradition, he'd told Aladdin when he was a small child. To have the gift to add such flavours to meals was a magic of its own. A little could go a long way for the poor. To bring joy to many, that was his way, and while he might not have been rich, he had a wealth of friends who often brought honey cakes and other sweet treats for their favourite sellers. He told Aladdin that he too would know this joy when he was old enough to take over the business and have a family of his own. He said this when Aladdin was five and too young to know better. By the time Aladdin was eleven his disappointed – and perhaps heartbroken – father had realised that this lazy son of his would never amount to much and, were he to inherit the

3

business, would either run it into the ground or sell it on.

And now Aladdin was fifteen, even though he looked younger, and he knew what his father and mother had never realised. He wasn't lazy. He was simply differently gifted.

Yes, he decided, as the guard let out another pig-like grunt, this man did remind him of his father. It made his decision easy.

In a swift move, he pulled his sharp blade across the man's thick neck, too fast for him to even startle. It was a quick and silent death, and very unlike the one he'd given his father a year or so ago. That had been a much messier affair, as had his mother's. But still, he thought, as he let himself in through the door to the Viceroy of the Meridien Isles' opulent living quarters, they had been his first. He'd got better since then.

He wiped the blade clean on his wet shorts and set about his task without another thought for the dead guard and his dreams.

Two

It was a warm day, and, once the door had appeared and she felt the full impact of the scent of the plants and flowers that surrounded the white tower, Rapunzel almost smiled with pleasure but then checked herself, keeping her back straight, and expression haughty. Icy and aloof. That was all she would ever show to a visitor, especially a man. Her Aunt Gretel had taught her well. That didn't stop Conrad's round and red face beaming at her as he did every time he paid them a visit.

'I've got some fine strawberries growing in my garden, so I put some in for your aunt,' he said.

'She probably won't eat them.'

'Well, maybe she will, and maybe she won't. They're a gift. Better than wasting them.' Conrad's eyes always shone with goodness and warmth, however rude Rapunzel was to him. And she was more often than not rude. Or at the very least indifferent. She excelled at indifference.

'Maybe one day she'll come down here again herself. Would be nice to see her.'

'Highly unlikely.' Rapunzel took the basket of chopped pieces of ash and maple from him, topped with the sack of food items Aunt Gretel had requested. Two rabbits, some fish and a fine cake from the baker. Aunt Gretel had a sweet tooth.

'Is that everything?' He'd been paid when they'd placed the order and there was really no need for him to loiter.

'Got something for you too. It's under all that wood.' He winked at her, almost fatherly, his eyes twinkling. Rapunzel had often wondered where he found so much humour. 'Can't read myself, but I figure a well-brought up girl like yourself can manage letters. I saw the cover and thought you might like it.'

'Thank you,' she muttered, not really sure what else to say. She had plenty of books. Books about science, books detailing the history of the kingdoms, books listing the plants and herbs growing in the forests, books about magic and dragons, books about animals. What other kind of books did she need?

'See you next week,' she added, a last-minute impetuous comment, and Conrad, already returning to his horse and cart carrying last week's empty basket, raised one hand and waved in farewell.

Rapunzel stepped back and as soon as she was clear of the doorway, the door itself vanished, eaten up by the wall, only smooth stone visible where the heavy wood had been moments ago. While this might be a thing of wonder to those who lived in the village, to Rapunzel it was simply the front-door-that-mainly-wasn't-there, which, when she thought about it logically, was probably the best kind of door to have. Doors that were there all the time were far easier for the outside world to find a way through, and if there was one thing her Aunt Gretel didn't like it was the outside world.

She hitched the basket to the metal hook hanging on a long rope, and then ran up the winding staircase to the next landing, taking the stone steps two at a time, her long, slim legs enjoying the challenge. When she'd been younger she'd run all the way up and down the tower over and over, just for the fun of it, but now the tower was bigger and there were more rooms and plenty of space for her to dance and do cartwheels and play act, even though she was twenty-one and too old for such things.

When she got to the first landing she cranked the handle set into the wall and the basket rose up towards her. She stored the food in the pantry, which was always much cooler than the rest of the tower, and then took the next three flights up, past her aunt's bedroom nestled amongst the doors and corridors in the centre of the tower. The structure narrowed the higher she went. She turned another handle in the wall and the basket followed her up and she carried it into the large room that was her bedroom and also served as her workshop.

The wood was all well cut and pliable and she laid it out neatly by type ready to carve and cut and smooth and join together. She'd made so many spinning wheels she could probably build one in her sleep. She looked back into the basket. There was the book, just as Conrad had promised, but it did not look like any volume she'd seen before. It was smaller than the dark and heavy thickly-bound leather tomes in Aunt Gretel's study and the cover was brightly covered and at the centre was a beautiful girl in a fine dress, held in a very handsome man's arms.

'Rapunzel?'

She quickly stuffed the ridiculous looking book under her straw mattress and hurried up the final flight of steps to Aunt Gretel, in her potion room. It

8

was stuffy and warm as usual, with several candles burning for light in the gloom. There were only two windows in the white tower that was their world, one in the kitchen, and one in Rapunzel's room to let the wood dust escape when she was working, and of course for that *other* activity that brought them both so much entertainment.

'Did Conrad bring everything we need?' Her aunt didn't turn as she finished applying a drop of dark liquid to the pin of a spindle and placed it down carefully to dry before replacing the stopper on the small vial and putting it back in her cabinet.

'Yes. And he brought you some strawberries from his garden.'

'The man's a fool.' Aunt Gretel snorted with derision. 'He thinks I'm lonely. Always has.' She sat down heavily in her rocking chair, the lines around her mouth pulling into a frown. Her waist and hips had thickened slightly over the years, and on another woman it might serve to make them seem warmer and more feminine, but Aunt Gretel's cold stare combined with her ice-white hair put paid to any hint of that.

'Because he's a man,' Rapunzel said, her beautiful face twisting into an unpleasant smirk. 'And men are cruel or stupid or, most often, both.'

'Good girl.' Aunt Gretel nodded, pleased, before frowning again. 'Where are your shoes? Did you speak to him barefoot?'

Rapunzel looked down, her face reddening. 'Sorry, Auntie. It's easier to run down the steps without them.'

'I've told you many times, dear. Make them wait. And always look perfect. Perfect and unattainable. That's the way to keep them weak. To break a man's heart without so much as touching him. Make them fear you for simply being yourself.'

'It was only Conrad,' Rapunzel said quietly. She didn't like disappointing her Aunt Gretel. 'He's an old man.'

'He's forty-five, I think. Not that much older than me. Although of course he will grow old much quicker than I. Witches live a very long time.'

Rapunzel said nothing. Both her aunt and Conrad seemed ancient to her.

'And he loves you, I'm sure,' Gretel smiled. 'How could he not? You're twenty-one years old and so very beautiful.' There was an edge in her voice – a hunger, perhaps – whenever she mentioned Rapunzel's beauty that left the young woman slightly uneasy. Was she beautiful? She had very little to compare herself with except the occasional country maid who wandered too close to the tower. They tended to hurry back into the forest, hiding their faces under their caps; the tales of the witch in the tower were enough to keep most of the surrounding villagers at bay. Mainly, their visitors, other than Conrad, were fat pigeons carrying messages, or servants coming to collect secretly ordered items. The only times men came themselves to ask for Aunt Gretel's help was when they feared their pigeons would be intercepted. It seemed to Rapunzel that no one could be trusted at all, in the Nine Kingdoms. Not even kings and queens.

Rapunzel left Aunt Gretel to her work and went to the kitchen to make them both a rabbit stew, enjoying the summer breeze. She felt unsettled. She'd felt unsettled quite a lot recently, the tower walls becoming somewhat stifling. Perhaps that's why she hadn't shown Aunt Gretel the book Conrad had given her. They would usually laugh at the stupid man and his stupid presents, but today she wanted something of her own. For herself.

Sometimes – although she was sure Aunt Gretel loved her in her own way – she felt she only existed as an extension of her aunt's wishes. Not that she minded too much. From everything Aunt Gretel had told her and shown her in books of war and murder throughout the kingdoms, wars so bad that even the dragons had returned to the Far Mountain and rarely danced and sang in the skies anymore, men really were terrible creatures to be avoided at all costs and the outside world left little to be desired.

No, she told herself as she skinned the rabbit, she was content with her life. She would stay in the tower, and when she was older and had white hair, she'd find a fresh girl to make the spinning wheels and she'd use Aunt Gretel's store of potions and pretend to be a witch herself. She would live in the tower for ever. The tower was safe.

The day passed in their usual pattern of work and food and then studying in the library, Aunt Gretel quizzing her on the rarest plants in the forest and what spices to blend them with to add nuance to any spell. A love spell was no use without specifics, as many fools had learned. What kind of love was required? From who? Did you want a painful death for an enemy or an easy one for a loved one? Every type of magic had its own scent and flavour, and each required a delicate touch when dripped onto the wood. One drop too many could change everything.

There were two powers women had in the world, her Aunt Gretel had often told her. Magic and beauty. She had one, and Rapunzel had the other. Rapunzel had insisted cleverness must be a power but her aunt had just laughed at that. *Only if you have one of the other two*, she'd replied. *If not, then to be clever as a woman is a curse. Men will not thank you for it.*

Only when she finally lay down on her small bed for the night, moonlight streaming bright across the floor, did she pull the strange volume out from under her mattress and look at it properly. The beautiful couple on the cover were dressed so finely it rang a chord deep inside her, and her head suddenly whirled with fabrics of a hundred different colours, and brightly lit ballrooms, and so many people it made her dizzy, the tinkle of another girl's laugh, and then – as ever – a man in a crimson jacket.

She blinked and the images vanished.

These snatches of memory made her feel strange. Everything from before the tower was a blur. Sometimes, if she tried really hard, she would remember how much she'd cried when she arrived, and how in the end her Aunt Gretel – not really her aunt at all – had given her a potion and the sadness had faded along with the memories of her past. Now it was just them – and she was content with that.

She rarely even looked at the tattered piece of parchment the crimson jacket-clad man – her father, she *knew* he was her father – had left tucked into her shoe, that Aunt Gretel had never known about. *I love*

13

you with all my heart and I promise I'll come back for you soon. Papa. That's all it said.

Well, he *hadn't* come back, and that, along with everything Aunt Gretel and her books had told her about the cruelty of men was all Rapunzel needed to know about love. Even fathers couldn't be trusted.

She looked back down at the cover of the strange book. How could the beautiful girl be gazing at the man like that, even if, she had to admit, he was very handsome? Surely all girls out in the world knew how awful men were? What on earth could there be to like about them?

She got out of bed, took her pillow and sat under the windowsill, the moon brighter than any reading candle, and, only to satisfy her curiosity that this really would be the most ridiculous story, she started to read.

It was a world of balls and fantastic clothing and expensive carriages and, somehow, she knew what all these things were as if deep down in her memory they had once been a part of her life. As she turned the pages, the room around her faded and she was lost in the world within the words, entranced by the tale.

It was nearly dawn when she reluctantly put the book down with a third of the story still to go. Every inch of her skin was flushed and even though her aunt

14

would be up in an hour or so and their day would begin, and she really should at least close her eyes, she wasn't sure she could sleep at all. What had she just read? The princess and the blacksmith – well, the things they'd done with their clothes off. When she'd read how they touched each other her body tingled so much she wanted to run her hands over it and touch wherever the blacksmith was touching in the book. She felt on fire.

She'd had moments like this over the past few years, urges she didn't understand that left her most flustered and wanting to wash in cold water, but now she understood what they were. The need to kiss and touch and be touched. Her head was spinning.

Why had Aunt Gretel left all this out when she'd talked about the battles between men and women? She'd explained to Rapunzel that mating led to procreation. All of *that* was in the science books and had sounded quite revolting – having a person growing inside you and having to push it out and look after it while the man carried on with life as before – and another reason to live happily in the tower as her aunt had chosen to, but this was something quite different. This wasn't mating for mating's sake. This was – well, she flushed a little deeper – this was something she thought she'd quite *like*. If even half of what she'd read in Conrad's book was true then sometimes the battleground of men and women could lead to something quite magical in itself, whether you were a witch or a princess or a milkmaid.

She got to her feet and stood in front of the window, the fresh early breeze delicious as it caressed her through her nightdress, teasing every inch of her skin. Her breath caught as the air found its way between her legs. Suddenly she felt like a woman, not a girl, and she closed her eyes and danced with the breeze, as if she was the princess at the ball, dancing with the prince, and knowing the blacksmith was waiting outside the castle, hoping she'd choose him.

Courtly music played in her head, the fantasy dredging lost memories to the surface as she twirled in front of the window. It was only when she heard low voices drifting up that she stopped, panting, her reverie broken.

The sun was coming up, and in the streaking pale yellow glow past the rich gardens of flowers and herbs at the edge of the forest, she could make out four figures – young men – looking up at her. She leaned out, her long, golden hair, having come loose as she danced, trailing part way down the smooth white wall, and the tingle on her skin started up again as she studied them.

Their words didn't carry, but she could hear their voices, deep and masculine, and they stood tall with broad chests beneath white shirts and their doublets undone, or slung over one shoulder. When they realised they'd been seen, the most confident of the four stepped forward and she saw that while they were handsome, they were also drunk and veering on boorish as they grinned up at her, swaying and leaning on each other.

'Come down here and dance with me!' the tallest and perhaps the leader of this merry band called up to her, his hands planted on his hips, standing with his legs wide. 'We'll get a sweat on, that much is certain.'

He looked back at his friends who laughed, and as she saw their crudeness the heat from her skin vanished. Did they think they could impress her so easily? Despite how she'd lost herself in Conrad's book, all the teachings from her aunt had been imprinted on her for years and this arrogance only made her all the more full of disdain for these foolish boys. She smiled coquettishly, twirling a strand of hair.

'Oh, I wish I could, but until someone rescues me I'm trapped in here. For, you see, I've been cursed to stay locked in this tower all my life by a wicked witch.' She leaned further out, knowing that even from that far below the young men would have a tantalising glimpse of her cleavage. 'She has a room full of magic spindles and cursed spinning wheels and there are some that might kill you – or worse – should you touch them. And the only way to open the door, is to promise that you will each take your chance with a spindle. Am I worth that? For a dance?'

She watched as their confidence began to ebb away. At first they laughed, and then glanced at each other, none wanting to go first.

'Surely a witch and the risk of death doesn't scare you?' she called down to them as they backed away. 'To free me? But we must act quickly. For soon the witch will awaken and her vengeance on you for talking to me will be great. She turned the last man she caught into a toad.'

It came as no surprise to her when they started to back away. Most men were cowards, as Aunt Gretel had always said.

'We are headed to the Eastern Seas to take up life on the ships,' the tallest of them, not so cocky now, called up, in a much more hushed tone, as he sought cover under the canopy of the trees. 'But we will come back for you. We promise!'

Rapunzel's smile turned into an unpleasant sneer, and she went back inside and flopped on her bed, all thoughts of princes and blacksmiths forgotten. The promises of men, as she'd learned from her own father, weren't worth the parchment they were written on.

Three

The salmon in the river were notoriously difficult to catch for most of the villagers, but Conrad's nets always provided two or three large fish to eat or sell, and it made him think that Gretel the witch was fonder of him than she allowed herself to believe, because everybody knew that water and witches went together, and this river ran right under the white tower. If Gretel thought him the nuisance she claimed then he would catch no fish at all.

Thinking of Gretel and young Rapunzel locked up in that impenetrable tower gave him a wave of sadness that even the beautiful early morning couldn't dispel. He'd been emptying his hare traps when the group of drunken young men had gone by, and he'd heard them laughing at how scared they'd been by the threat of the witch made by the trapped beauty, joking about who had been the most cowardly and how would they survive on the Eastern Seas.

Like the rest of the village, Conrad could never quite remember how Rapunzel had come to be in the tower or when she'd arrived. It felt like she'd been there for ever, and that with every season that passed, she was turning into a copy of her aunt – cold and haughty and with a disdain for love and romance and men, all the magic and mess that came with simply being alive. He'd heard the stories of how Gretel had come to build the tower here, and if they were even half true then he couldn't blame her for disliking men, but if Gretel was beyond hope – and he didn't believe she was, being someone who always tried to see the positive in every situation – he didn't want the same for Rapunzel. She was a beautiful young woman and this life was unfair on her. That's why he'd given her the book. It had cost him dearly at the market, but the trader had grinned and said that the story would certainly make the reader crave love, and so he thought it worth the piece of silver he'd parted with. His shoes could go without being cobbled for a while longer. The forest floor was mainly soft and the weather was mild.

By the time he'd got back to his cabin at the edge of the village the sun was high, the bees were buzzing in the hives, and the scent of fresh blooms welcomed him from his tended gardens. He wished that Gretel would see them one day. The sight might bring her some joy. Perhaps he'd cut some flowers for Rapunzel to give to her aunt the next time he took their provisions.

He sighed and brought up a bucket of cold spring water from the well and drank a long cup. It was promising to be another warm day and it was hard to stay gloomy. It would all work out well. The right young man would come along for Rapunzel in the end and he would persevere past her disdain. The young woman deserved some romance. She should know love. They all should, he decided, as he went inside his empty cottage. Maybe one day even he would have that joy. He chuckled a little at that, knowing his bow legs and simple life didn't exactly make him a catch. But as with all things, Conrad was an optimist.

Four

The young king had to admit he was rather enjoying Port Sinbad, even if his cousin, the duke, who
was asleep beside him on a chair, his tightly coiled
curls and dark skin still sand-dusted from wrestling
pirates for sport, was wearying of sore heads and late
nights. The king couldn't entirely blame him. Whereas
the young king's youth as the only son of an elderly
ruler had been rigid and dry and formal, the duke
had enjoyed plenty of adventures already and knew
the lands well, which in part was why the ministers
of the Kingdom of the High Born had agreed to this
secret trip at all. As far as the subjects of his homeland
were concerned the young king was in mourning
for his father, the old king, and was locked away in
the contemplation room high in a turret of the castle

that few ever knew about or could even find the way to.

He leaned forward and took a fresh oyster from the duke's plate and washed it down with some dwarf beer, something that never found its way to his own kingdom where wine was the drink of the wealthy and mead the drink of the poor.

He was a sensory man and this was a sensory place, and as the sun set and the air grew heavier and more humid, he took in a deep breath, enjoying the myriad scents carried from the markets that filled so many of the streets. His journey was coming to an end, and while he looked forward to all the pleasures being king would bring, he'd be sad to leave all this behind. Especially when he was yet to have the adventure he'd truly craved.

Beside him the duke let out a small snore, and the young king smiled. They had had their fair share of fun, that was for sure, even if his own itch wasn't completely satisfied.

None of his advisors had been happy that he'd wanted to explore the Nine Kingdoms so soon after taking the throne, but he'd persuaded them there would never be a better time. It was summer, the crops were plentiful, and the kingdoms were – for once – relatively at peace. No armies were being sent to the Battle Lands, so it was unlikely they'd be set upon by men returning home still filled with blood lust. So travel he had, and here he was.

He'd known from lessons with his father's ministers that the Kingdom of the Eastern Seas was a melting pot where all the kingdoms traded in the bright sunshine and sandy warmth, but books and the words of dry old men, who'd probably never left the castle grounds for years let alone their own kingdom, could not adequately describe the *life* here. The Eastern Seas was a fascinating place – a long but narrow stretch of land that was the only part of the coastline where the seas met the earth without hindrance of sinking sands or the troll rocks that posed such danger for inexperienced sailors or those thrown off course by storms – and all along the white shores were markets and harbours and trading posts where anything and could be bought from and sold by all manner of people, often with no questions asked. He was very glad that their journey had brought them here.

He loved the sense of freedom that came with the heat. No one wore thick doublets here, but floaty shirts of the lightest fabrics, and boots were replaced with sandals. The only item of clothing the young king wore that gave away his own status was the gold buckle on his belt, which bore the insignia of his kingdom – a lit torch shining through a golden crown, the crown inlaid with diamonds indicating he was no mere knight or nobleman but the king himself. While he didn't mind being *almost* incognito, he never wanted to be mistaken for a common man.

As he drank more dwarf beer, eating the dried meats and figs and olives and pastries that were no doubt the cause of his royal belt feeling slightly tighter, his companion finally stirred, yawning loudly beside him, before rubbing his face and sitting up straighter.

'You slept for two whole hours,' the young king said with a grin. 'It's almost ten.'

'Please tell me we're not going to drink away another night. I don't think there's an ale maid left in this kingdom you haven't taken your fill of, from both her tray and her bodice.' He leaned forward and drank from the water jug before tearing off a piece of bread. 'We'll have to send a ship out to the Barbaric Lands to find some pale, sharp-teethed, untamed women to please you.' He chuckled and the young king joined in. He had not been shy about satisfying his needs and wants, that was for sure.

'It's all right, my friend, I know you're weary and want to return home.'

'I can't lie, that is the truth. It has been several weeks and I miss my wife, and our child will be born soon.'

'It will be a handsome, healthy boy, I'm sure.' The young king loved his cousin, who had always been more like an older brother to him, and he didn't want to make him unhappy. 'But you're right. You should be with your wife. I've kept you away for long enough.'

His own queen-to-be was waiting patiently – or perhaps not so patiently – at his castle. She was a beautiful and demure princess from the Kingdom of Nature's Keep, who would provide him with heirs and comfort and never cause her husband to raise his voice to her. In many ways, he knew the marriage was ideal, but he was in no hurry to race back to such domesticity.

'Should we leave in the morning?' the duke asked, suddenly alert and fully awake, and it was clear that he, on the other hand, was excited by the prospect of home.

'*You* should.' The words came out before the king had really thought them through, but as soon as he'd spoken his plan was set. 'Go back and tell them to start the royal wedding preparations. I will be home in two weeks.'

'I can't go back without you,' the duke said, alarmed. 'My duty is to keep you safe.'

'Your duty was to guide me on our travels. And that you have done! We have travelled far, with tales to tell of trying to scale the sheer side of the Far Mountain but being forced back by the heat of *dragon* breath. Of finding an enchanted thicket so high that we couldn't climb it, the branches threatening to trap us inside when we tried to cut through. Of witnessing a witch burning in the Winter Lands . . . you were my companion for it all.'

A thin, blind beggar dressed in rags shuffled past and the young king tossed him a silver coin and his companion the remains of the loaf of bread. The beggar scrabbled for both, and then sat on his haunches in the shadows of the tavern awning, tearing at the bread with his teeth.

'But I need something more,' the king continued, 'something new. The kind of adventure they will write songs about. I need a chivalrous challenge. A beautiful damsel in distress, maybe.' He did want those things, yes, but perhaps, if he was honest, what he wanted was something that wasn't quite as *easy* as his life had been thus far. A woman who wasn't quite as obtainable as the stream of willing bedfellows happy to succumb to his handsome good looks and silver coin.

The beggar nodded thanks in their direction and scurried away, head down under a filthy cowl.

'I cannot leave you behind alone,' the duke replied.

'Your ministers would send me to the Troll Road for it.'

'There are soldiers for hire here. I've seen plenty. Perhaps we can pay some to protect me from a distance. And I will give you a letter declaring that you have returned on orders from your king and no one is to harm you or punish you for it. Will that suffice?'

The night crickets began to chirp, loud and merry in the marginally cooler air, and at their feet, in the pool of light from the hanging lantern above them, flying ants settled like a carpet. The young king watched the revulsion on his friend's face and he knew the lure of their temperate home with its clear, crisp air would win.

'If you insist,' the duke said, with a smile.

'I do,' the young king replied, and held up his tankard of dwarf beer. 'I also insist on saying a proper farewell.' As if by magic, two more tankards appeared, carried by two red-headed, brown-eyed beauties, who smiled in tandem at both young men. 'Twins,' the king said, taking in their curves. '*That* would be new.'

Five

Bread had never tasted so good, Aladdin decided as he slipped the silver coin into his pocket and finished the last of the loaf, starving despite the nausea that had been his companion in the dark throughout his long day of hiding in the broken barrel in the corner of the docks. The wood had been covered in the slime and stench of rotten fish made worse by the heat of the day, and he'd breathed it in between careful sips of water from his gourd, forced to listen to the chatter and wild tales of all the foolish young men queuing up to sign on for the peacekeeper and trader ships, while waiting for the soldiers to tire of their hunt. It had been a very long wait for night to fall once more.

His legs were still painfully stiff, but his awkward walk helped with his hunched disguise, and with the rags he'd stolen from a sleeping beggar, no one would recognise him as the agile youth he was. He moved, unnoticed through the narrow winding streets of Sinbad, until he came to the home of his patron.

There were two guards dressed all in black at the entrance who blocked his way with large scimitars until he whispered his name and they let him pass, but not before he saw a hint of disgust flash across one guard's face.

The narrow jetty was lined with lit torches and the floating palace, one so luxurious that perhaps even the Emperor of the Eastern Seas himself envied it, sat a hundred feet from the shore, gold-gilded domes and mosaic tiled turrets, all lit up with mineral lamps burning in all the colours of the rainbow.

At the end of the jetty he pushed back his cowl and trotted up the marble steps, the exercise having finally eased out the aches in his slim legs, and, as they always did, the heavy arched wooden doors swung open before he'd pulled on the bell cord.

Inside, the vast cool atrium smelled of sandalwood and musk, and water trickled from the carved statue in the corner, loud in the silence, running into the lagoon pool that was a border around the edges in which iridescent fish darted this way and that. Aladdin didn't like to admit it but as he waited there, bare feet on the smooth tiles, he was somewhat nervous. What had been fun at the time was probably about to have repercussions.

When no one came to fetch him, he crept further into the palace, half-expecting a servant to appear at any corner and take him back to the atrium to wait, but none did. Perhaps the Great Magician didn't trust his servants not to share Aladdin's whereabouts. His palm was sweaty around the black-pearl necklace. At least he'd completed his task. The magician couldn't complain about that.

As he grew closer to the magician's study, he heard the murmurings of voices, one he recognised – the magician's own – and another, deeper and resonant with an echoey timbre, as if it came from deep within a cave. 'But remember, Master, to try to profit from murder with magic can be a trap.'

Instead of knocking, he peered through the gap in the door. The magician, dressed in fine, red silk robes, looked tiny next to his companion, a huge, thick-armed man who wore a waistcoat over his deep bronze, naked, muscled torso and balloon trousers, the sort that were the fashion maybe a hundred years ago. His hair was long and dark, hanging all the way down to his feet. The magician muttered something Aladdin didn't catch.

'As you wish, Master,' the other said, and then with an electric crack, like lightning striking the Far Mountain, he disappeared into a puff of red smoke and swirled down into the spout of a small, tarnished lamp. Aladdin had to stop himself from gasping. A genie. The magician had a *genie*. He'd heard rumours they existed but, like the dragons, sightings were rare. Aladdin's eyes narrowed as he watched the magician lock the small lamp in an onyx cupboard and put the key on a chain safely back around his neck and under his robes.

A genie. Aladdin's mouth watered with a different kind of greed. He could have everything he ever desired if he could get his hands on that lamp. All as easily as making a wish. But procuring the lamp somehow would have to wait. First, he needed to get out of his current predicament.

Aware that the magician knew he was in the house, he delayed no longer and knocked on the door, his heart racing as he stepped inside.

'I have the item you requested,' he said, bowing low even though he loathed the self-styled Great Magician with more emotion than he usually found himself capable, and then held up the string of rare, black pearls, farmed from poisonous oysters deep under the coral reefs that surrounded the furthest of the Meridien Isles, that he'd retrieved from the viceroy's treasure ship. They glowed from within like hot coals, full of the promise of magic, and he'd made sure to wipe them clean of blood before he'd tucked them into his leather pouch and swum for shore.

There was a swirl of red silk and then the pearls were snatched from his fingers just before the wind was knocked from his chest and he found himself pressed up against the wall, held by nothing but air, the Great Magician holding out a bright blue wand in his direction.

'I told you to steal them,' the magician hissed angrily. 'Not murder the viceroy and his entire family and crew. I'm told it was a bloodbath. How much attention did you need? If you've been followed and brought soldiers to my door then I will wear your skin as a suit, boy.'

Struggling to get a breath, and trying to wriggle free from the magical pressure that held him so tightly, Aladdin wanted to say the magician should go on a diet for a while first if that was his plan, but he was glad that the words were silenced by his somewhat more urgent need to stay alive. The magician was clearly in no mood for his sharp observations.

'The pearls were in a vault.' His words were barely there, the husk of a whisper. 'And I had to get the key, which was in a sealed pocket in his nightshirt. Then his wife woke up. And then she screamed. So, what else was I to do?'

If he could have shrugged he would have and, thankfully, after a very long moment when it felt as if the pressure was increasing, he fell with a thud to the floor, where he stayed, gasping for air. This was not turning out to be his finest day. While having the Great Magician as a patron could work in his favour, he was very aware that the man's tendency to take pleasure in violence was second only to his own.

'I should have you flogged,' the magician hissed. 'Or lock you up downstairs with the others who've crossed me. Maybe I'll leave you there to starve and listen until your screams turn to sobs and you beg for your life.'

'I'm sorry – I—' He'd come with the pearls expecting the three gold coins he'd been promised and a few sharp words, and now he realised he'd be lucky to escape with his life. He sometimes forgot how unacceptable most people found murder.

'What is your apology worth? You're useless to me now. Everyone in the kingdom is looking for you. What you failed to realise in your blood frenzy is that a young servant was hidden in a closet and you missed him. There's now a reward on your head, Aladdin.

The emperor takes his relationship with the Meridien Isles very seriously. What if someone connects you to me?' He turned away, and muttered, 'Perhaps I should wish you dead,' and his hand went to his neck where the key to the onyx cupboard sat.

Having seen the genie, the words filled Aladdin with dread and he scrabbled forward across the floor and held his patron's ankle. A thought struck him as he wracked his fevered brain for something – anything – he could use to get himself out of this mess. A story he'd heard while he was trapped in the stinking barrel, told by a few loud young men waiting to take to the seas. 'What if I can bring you a dozen magic spindles? Maybe more? A room full of them?'

He looked up, his eyes pleading and pitiful, while his sly brain calculated his chances of reprieve. While his patron might *call* himself the Great Magician, as far as Aladdin knew, if you really *were* something you didn't need to shout about it. And often didn't want to. He knew that he himself was an exceptional assassin – the missed servant aside – but it would hardly be good for business if that was what he called himself. He suspected this 'great' magician had no magic of his own, but knew only how to wield the magical items of others. It was his collection that was great, and claiming the title for himself was basically a challenge to every thief in the kingdom. He was a vain fool.

The magician's eyes narrowed. 'Is this one of your tall stories?'

'No. I promise.' Aladdin pulled himself up on his knees, not missing the flash of greed on the magician's face. 'I'd have to leave the kingdom to get them, but I can do that, and by the time I return all this will be forgotten. Or at least my part in it will. And I'm sure there are plenty of young boys who look enough like me that one could be arrested in my place. As for the spinning wheels, I have a plan. I was going to tell you about them but – well, I didn't have a chance.'

'A room full, you say?'

Aladdin nodded and allowed himself a small smile. 'All laced with magic. Each with its own curse or charm.'

The magician sat down in his ornately carved and velvet-cushioned chair. He reached across and took a large slice of cheese from a plate stacked high with delicacies. 'Then fetch them for me,' he said, with his mouth full. 'And when you do there will be ten gold coins in it for you. Enough to send you on your way. Perhaps you could work in the spice markets like your father did.' He spoke even as he ate and flecks of cheese came out with his words, as he amused himself with the thought.

'Perhaps I will,' Aladdin said, with another deep bow. 'Thank you, my patron.' He backed out, bent low, as if the magician were the emperor, and made a quiet promise to himself that when this job was done, he'd kill the magician, too.

Six

The young king wasn't sure if it was the fresh morning air, cooled under the canopy of the forest, or if it was the excitement of his chivalric adventure, but he felt better than he deserved to given the amount he'd drunk the night before. He'd been sad to say goodbye to the duke and had momentarily wondered if it was foolhardy not to go home with him.

He'd sat, quite melancholy, skin pale under his thick, dark hair, at their usual table looking out over the hazy, glittering water, not even the ale maids able to cheer him, and that was when the boy had approached him. He was wearing the colours of the king's homeland, the Kingdom of the High Born, sky-blue knickerbockers and a matching gold-trimmed waistcoat over his coarse shirt. He told the king they'd been given to him by his dead father who had moved to the Eastern Seas as a child himself but had dreamed of home until his dying day, and after that they'd bonded.

And now here they were, heading for an adventure. At first he couldn't quite believe the story of the beautiful girl trapped by a wicked witch, but the boy told it in such detail and with such wide-eyed honesty that he found himself becoming excited at the prospect of finding out for himself. It was fortuitous – or even perhaps fate – that the boy had heard this tale while cleaning boots at the dock and also heard that there was a nobleman in Sinbad seeking an adventure. Yes, he decided, as he ducked under a branch as the forest thickened around them and the path narrowed, it was fate that had brought him here. A damsel in distress. A heroic quest.

The boy was walking ahead, their limited provisions in the king's own saddlebags, but the young king wasn't worried that they would get lost or go without, even though they had perhaps another day or two of travelling before they were close to the tower. He had his bow and arrow and had always proved excellent in the hunt, and the boy was keeping them close to the stream, which – if the young sailors yarn was to be believed – would lead them in the right direction, so they would not be without fresh water. Also, he knew something the boy did not – that there were six hired soldiers following not so far behind, who would be with them in an instant were any danger to befall them. He had almost told Aladdin, but decided against it. The boy might not understand that a king always had to have a guard with them and would think him a coward or weak, and that would not do at all.

He let his mind wander pleasantly as they continued at a steady but not tiring pace, enjoying the cooler air away from the shores of the Eastern Seas. What would she be like, this fair maiden of the tower? Beautiful, no doubt, otherwise she would not have made such an impression on the travelling men. What must her life have been like, locked up for ever by a witch? Had she had many suitors? How lonely must she be? It was refreshing to have so many questions. The women he'd bedded on this trip so far had all had their share of charms, and he could harden just thinking about some of his exploits, but none had intrigued him like this tale of the maiden in the tower. The thrill of a witch and threat of magic. He smiled to himself, in his mind's eye already the hero of the day.

***

Aladdin had always preferred the hustle and bustle of the busy cities to the quiet of the forest, but it was a relief to be away from Sinbad and the worry of reward-hunters scooping him up and delivering him to the emperor. Even with his hair cut short and in his new clothes, he hadn't relaxed until the canopy folded over them and he was sure they were alone. Well, alone except for the six soldiers following them, who were a headache he'd have to deal with at some point before going back to Sinbad to make sure they didn't sell him to the emperor and claim the reward themselves. Which, to be fair, was exactly what he would do in their position, and exactly why he was going to have to slit their throats.

As he picked up his pace, he adjusted his uncomfortable trousers. He'd bought the clothes with the sixpence his companion had thrown at him, his magpie eyes having spied the young king's golden belt buckle. A tailor in the market had told him which kingdom it was from and that the diamonds meant he was royalty, and so he'd found an outfit and created a story about its origin that would make the young king trust him. Aladdin might not be a magician or a witch, but he understood people, which was a magic of its own. He could make someone trust him without even realising why, and that's what he'd done to the young king.

People gravitated towards their own, and the people of the Eastern Seas knew that better than most, for while it was a melting pot, each coastal area had its own tribes and customs, and that was how their leader had styled himself an emperor when there was no empire at all.

Also, the title kept them free from invasion in the main part, for it promised a greater army than perhaps the emperor had. He'd also made clear that the Eastern Seas were not to be crossed, because they did not follow the other kingdoms' chivalric code of going to the Battle Lands should they want a war. The tribes of the Eastern Seas were easy-going and tolerant, but if under threat, they had proved they would take the fight to the kingdoms and their people, and no king really had a hunger for that. Aladdin found, as he walked through the unfamiliar greenery of the forest, that he felt quite proud of his homeland and his emperor, even if he never wanted to meet him face-to-face.

If this plan paid off, he thought, as he glanced back and gave a subservient smile to the king on his horse, then that would no longer be a worry. He'd steal the spinning wheels and spindles, say farewell to the king, kill the soldiers and then get back to the Great Magician who should have – if he kept his word – found someone else to pay the price for Aladdin's little murderous indiscretions on the viceroy's boat. Admittedly the whole 'steal the spindles' part of his plan was still a blank sheet, but he was good at thinking on his feet and he had the foolish but handsome young king – still vainly 'pretending' to be a nobleman while wearing his belt buckle – as a tool.

So far, he concluded, as the very tip of a white tower appeared in the distance in a gap in the canopy, things were going well. He'd be back in Sinbad for the genie and a life of riches in no time at all.

Seven

'There's nothing in any of our books about love,' Rapunzel said, when Aunt Gretel had finished washing, brushing and plaiting her long, golden hair that could probably hang halfway down the tower if it wasn't for Aunt Gretel's care and this once-a-week wash and redo.

She'd had to grit her teeth as her aunt tugged knots out of it, and she was sure there was magic at work in her hands because once it was plaited it was thick, but a normal length.

Sometimes Rapunzel wished she could just cut her hair off at her shoulders, but her aunt had told her it would grow until her father returned for her – and when it was free to cascade, it would be a reminder for her of the inconsistencies of men.

Rapunzel wondered if her aunt knew how cruel that was – to remind her of her abandonment – though it was clear that Aunt Gretel knew more of the dangers of men than Rapunzel and she was keeping her safe for a reason. But still, she thought as she sipped her warming glass of wine and browsed the high shelves, the book Conrad had given her had brought up a hundred questions that wouldn't go away however much she tried to dismiss them.

She had read it three times now, and each time it had the same effect of making her heart race and her skin flush, leaving her with such an ache of longing that even after she'd touched herself – several times – under her night dress, it still lingered. It wasn't just the physical acts in the book that were lurid, colourfully described and exhaustingly frequent, but the desire for love that went with them. In the story, everyone finally found their true love and lived happily ever after. How could such an outcome be possible if all men were wicked and selfish and not to be trusted?

Aunt Gretel looked up from her book, goblet of wine in hand, and an empty cake plate on the table beside her heavy, wooden reading chair, and frowned. 'Why would there be? There is nothing empirical or magical about love. If it even exists outside of a word utilised to gain selfish ends, which I very much doubt.' She paused to sip her wine. 'Except perhaps that of a mother's love, such as I have for you.'

'What about fathers?' Rapunzel lit another candle, even though perhaps fifteen already glowed around the room. She was finding the lack of windows in the tower more and more repressive, the air stifling in the warm nights despite the thick walls. 'Don't they love their children? And their wives?'

Gretel snorted derisively. 'Yours didn't come back. And you don't want to know about mine. A greedy man who would risk anything for wealth. My mother was too afraid of him to speak up so she withered and died of guilt. He did that to her. And your father and mine are not the exceptions. Love is a fickle and easily cast off ideal, Rapunzel. I've taught you this. The promise of it is used to hurt women. To subdue them and worse. You have to hurt men first. Keep your heart cold. That is how to survive in this world.' Her words were bitter – a reminder to Rapunzel that this was not Aunt Gretel's first goblet of wine this evening, and that she should tread carefully if she didn't want to be on the receiving end of one of her aunt's rants about the dangers of monstrous men.

'Why all these questions?' Aunt Gretel leaned

forward in her chair. 'This sudden interest in the foolishness of the heart? The great downfall of our sex?'

'I'm sorry,' Rapunzel said, even though she felt ashamed not to push harder. 'I had a strange dream. Perhaps a memory of my life before.'

It was true, she did sometimes have such dreams, more so since she had read her secret book, of a glittering life and beautiful people and laughter, but this time her words were a lie and she found it hard to look her aunt in the face as she spoke them, so she focused on the shelves instead, pretending to select a book. Her aunt was staring at her, she could feel it, and she wondered if perhaps her magic allowed her to sniff out a lie, so Rapunzel clapped her hands together and laughed, needing to distract her.

'Oh, I forgot to tell you!' She went to her aunt's chair and knelt on the floor at her feet, excited. 'Some foolish youths came by early in the morning a few days ago. Drunk and proud and stupid. They were clattering through the forest and woke me.'

Her aunt's eyes lit up slightly and she leaned forward. 'Go on.'

'They thought they were so big and clever.' Rapunzel laughed, a tinkle of broken glass, just like her aunt's was. 'I leaned out and let them see me. They started to strut, as they always do, and wanted me to come down and dance with them. But you'll never guess what I said to make them show their weakness.' She squeezed Aunt Gretel's knee. 'I said that I was the prisoner of a great witch with a room full of magical spindles and spinning wheels capable of doing great harm.'

'You're not exactly a prisoner, but the second part of that is true,' Aunt Gretel said.

'I know – it's what made it so convincing. And then I told the one that was preening at the front that I couldn't resist him, that I *could* come down and dance with him but only after he'd passed the witch's test. He'd have to randomly choose a spindle to be pricked by, risking his life, and that was the only way I could spend an evening with him.'

'Oh, that is delicious!' Aunt Gretel declared, laughing aloud. 'How perfect. Then what happened?'

'Well, they ran away, of course,' Rapunzel said with a delicate shrug. 'Because they were cowards.'

'As all men are in their shallow hearts,' her aunt added, and Rapunzel nodded. 'Although you should have given them time to consider before choosing. Three nights sounds better for curse breaking.' Her aunt was more relaxed after that and kept chortling to herself, amused by Rapunzel's clever thinking, and as she whiled away the hour until bedtime, pretending to study a text on the powers of mushrooms when mixed with thyme and two drops of witch's blood at a particular hour of night, Rapunzel couldn't wait to get to her room and read the book again.

Eight

Despite his lack of sleep, Conrad was bursting with joy as he got back to his cabin, the sun already warm and high in the sky, as if the day were celebrating the new birth too. His sister had almost given up hope that she and her husband, the baker, would be blessed with a child of their own. They had both been over thirty years when they wed and that was nearly ten years back, and while they loved each other very much it had been their great sorrow not to have a child. Then, when she'd fallen pregnant, every day had been a worry that either baby or mother or both might not survive, and while he feigned not worrying, even Conrad, with his natural optimism, had been kept awake in fear that it might all end badly.

But last night, the baby had arrived early, a healthy

– if small – baby boy, and both his sister and the infant were doing just fine. He had held the tiny child and cried with happiness and the excitement of someone new to love and share the world with. 'There's still time for you to have a family of your own,' the baker had said and that had been a bittersweet thought for Conrad. Although he worked with his hands, the baker's mind was sharp and Conrad could see that his brother-in-law knew that Conrad longed for a family of his own.

He lit the stove and put water on to boil for a nice cup of nettle tea, and while he waited, he thought about how small the baby had looked wrapped in the nursing blanket their mother had passed down to them before she died. He was a full six weeks early in the world and so while he looked well, could that be guaranteed for the future? He definitely needed a new and softer blanket than the one being used at the moment, and looking at his own bed, and the old goat hair blanket on it, he thought perhaps that Gretel and Rapunzel could reweave it and dye it bright colours for the boy, and perhaps even add a few drops of good health to the strands. It would make for a cold winter for him, but he could always find more wood for the stove, and he wanted nothing more than for his new nephew and his parents to be healthy and happy.

He folded up the blanket and then sat on his bed with his hot tea. Yes, he wanted to give this present to his family but how would he pay for it? However fond he was of Gretel and Rapunzel, he knew that Gretel would never gift magic or labour, not even to someone who had been visiting the tower all these years as he had. It would be silver or gold that she demanded and he had very little of either. He fed himself mainly from the land and sold his honey and the skins of the animals he caught in the forest – for while he did not have a huntsman's physique, he did have a huntsman's aim and affinity with nature – and what little coin he earned went on buying the necessities he could not provide for himself.

How could he make some money quickly, for every nursemaid who ever lived would say that the first few weeks of an infant's life were the most important if they were to do well in the world. He took the small jar from his bedside table and emptied it out on the mattress. There were two silver coins and three coppers. Nowhere near enough. He'd never asked for Gretel's magic before but he'd heard others in the village talking about what they'd paid and it was never less than two gold coins. Conrad couldn't remember when he'd last seen one gold coin, let alone two.

Still, he thought, as he carefully put his coins back,

he wouldn't give up hope. Something would come along. Life could be like that.

'Hello?' a male voice called from outside. 'Is there anyone home?'

Conrad got to his feet and hurried to the door, opening it to see a very handsome and finely dressed young man, with sharp cheekbones and dark, glossy hair, dismounting from a muscular stallion that was at least two hands too big to have been born in this part of the kingdoms. He appeared to be alone and his smile was open and friendly. As he came down the steps from his cabin, Conrad felt the sudden urge to doff his cap and bow his head, but he kept his chin up – this was his home after all – and returned the young gentleman's friendly smile.

'Are you lost?' he asked, the man's clothes and the slight lilt in his accent marking him as something of a foreigner. 'Have you come from the Eastern Seas?'

'I have,' the young man said. 'I've been travelling through the Nine Kingdoms and am on my way home to the Kingdom of the High Born. I'm looking for somewhere to rest for a few days. Can you tell me what kingdom this is?'

'Yes, young sir, I can. This is the Kingdom of Secrets Untold. No one knows why, but I suppose that's why the secrets are untold.' He laughed heartily at his own joke. 'But probably because the forest is full of secrets and people so often get lost here. And, if we have a king, none of us know who he is or where his castle might be. A collection of forest villages, that's what we are, living a simple life and we're happy for it. But apologies, I do witter on sometimes. If you're looking for lodgings, there's an inn in the village about half a mile that way,' Conrad nodded past the small daffodil patch that beamed sunshine back up at the sky. 'They might have a room or a barn you could use. Gets a bit noisy, mind.'

'I've had my fill of inns on my travels. And the headaches that accompany them, so I was looking for something a little quieter. I have gold coin. I can pay handsomely for a few days rest and food.'

'Well, I'm in need of two gold coins myself,' Conrad said, sending a silent prayer of thanks into the forest and the sky and to fortune herself. 'And while my cabin is not luxurious it is comfortable and the bed is clean. I can happily sleep in the chair by the fire and I am no nobleman's chef but my rabbit stew is second to none and I cook a fish well. My brother-in-law is the baker and there is fresh bread every day and a cake, if that's your fancy.'

'That will do very nicely. And in return, I can help you with your daily chores and chop wood for you. I would like to experience a few days of living close to nature before going back to the city.' He strode forward with a confidence Conrad had never seen in a village man, and as the visitor stood proud, Conrad spotted the gleaming belt buckle atop the man's breeches. A gold belt buckle with jewels encrusted on it? And that symbol. The crown and the flame.

Conrad rarely paid attention to news from beyond their quiet corner of the forest, as he had no need of the outside world and no hankering to see it, but he had a vague memory of gossip in the village that the old king from the Kingdom of the High Born had died and the young king was locked up in mourning. Jewels in a gold-crested belt buckle? He was a nobleman at the very least and looking at the way this young man stood – so confident and naturally proud – he would bet his meagre coins that this was the king himself, out for a last adventure before taking up the reins of power, as a young man with his whole life ahead of him should.

'Then this is a fine arrangement.' Conrad clapped him on his arm, for he was shorter than the young king and couldn't reach his shoulder, and led him inside. 'You shall be my guest and I hope you will leave with fond memories of your time here. And a full belly. Although,' he added, slapping his own round stomach, 'hopefully not quite so full as mine.' The young king laughed and Conrad decided that he liked him.

It was only later, after they'd eaten a lunch of bread, cheese and some cold duck with pickles his sister had given him, that a second thought came to Conrad. This was a young man who might be a king but who was clearly seeking something that he couldn't find in his homeland. Could that thing be true love? Could this be the man to make Rapunzel's icy heart melt? Surely Gretel wouldn't stop her young ward living the life of a queen? Conrad knew nothing of courtly ways, but he couldn't see how anyone would stand in the way of true love, and who would care if the king fell in love with a mysterious country girl? Love was surely all that mattered?

'Your timing has been most fortunate,' he said when they'd finished their repast. 'Now how do you feel about taking a walk with me through the forest? Good for the digestion and I need to take that blanket to the white tower. And maybe a couple of those delicious raspberry tarts.'

'I'll happily join you,' the young king said. 'But what is the white tower?'

'I'll explain all on the way,' Conrad said merrily, making sure the two gold coins the young king had already paid him were safely tucked into his pouch. 'It's quite the story. And let me do the talking when we get there. That's the best way until you know her better.'

'Her?'

'Like I said.' Conrad winked at him. 'I'll explain on the way.'

Nine

When Conrad rang the tower bell and Rapunzel idly glanced out of the window to see who was disturbing her work, she'd glimpsed his handsome companion and it took all her self-control not to run all the way down, barefoot and bodice loose, to open the door and get a closer look. Instead, she tightened her clothes, smoothed them, and put her daintiest shoes on, before quickly applying a little rose rouge to her cheeks and lips. Not that her cheeks needed it. She was quite flushed already.

He would be a disappointment, she told herself as she walked slowly down the spiral staircase, aware that Aunt Gretel was probably watching from the top to check her comportment. Yes, momentarily she'd thought the man from the front of the book Conrad had given her had magically sprung to life, but that was after a quick glimpse from a great height. No doubt he'd be thin and pasty and covered with boils when she opened the door. No real men were ever that handsome.

It turned out, as she opened the door and tried to maintain her icy, haughty stare, that some men really *were* that handsome. If anything, he was *more* handsome than the prince on the cover of her book. He had thick, black hair that almost curled and bright-blue eyes that shone out from tanned skin. He was broad and through his shirt she could see hints of well-shaped muscles in his strong arms. He was tall, but not too tall. Tall enough to have to bend to kiss her, she thought, and her cheeks prickled with a blush.

'Rapunzel, good day to you,' Conrad said, from his side of the doorway. His eyes, as ever, were twinkling, and she was sure that there was a touch of good-humoured amusement in them. Was her reaction to this stranger beside him so obvious?

'What do you want? You're not due for two days.' She was pleased at how cool and imperious her voice was. Sharp, almost. She did not look at the young man but cast her full displeasure at Conrad. 'I'm very busy.'

'My sister had a baby yesterday. Her first – and likely – only child. It came early and I'd like – if possible – to gift her a baby blanket infused with good health.' He held up a ratty old goat hair fleece. 'If you – or your Aunt Gretel – could weave one from this, I think I have enough to pay for it. I have two gold coins.'

Rapunzel stared at him and reluctantly took the blanket, nor sure she could deal with this new awkwardness in Conrad. She hadn't even known he had a family. He'd never mentioned a sister. And he'd certainly never asked for anything before.

'Her husband is the baker, and he made some fine tarts to celebrate. There are two here for your aunt.'

'I will pass on your request,' Rapunzel said. 'And tell you her decision when you come to collect our list of requirements in two days.' She was about to step back into the cool of the tower when she heard herself say, 'And who is this? Another of your relatives we know nothing about?'

She looked up at the young man then and her eyes confirmed once more what her racing heart was telling her. He really *was* extraordinarily handsome.

'Oh, just a travelling nobleman from a distant kingdom. He's staying for a few days and helping me with some tasks. And now we must get on,' Conrad said before she could ask anymore, or before the mysterious man could speak for himself, and then they'd turned and were walking away. The man glanced back at her for a moment, sending a thrill dancing across her skin, and then that was that. They were gone. She hadn't even heard him speak.

When she got back to the top of the stairs she found Aunt Gretel taking a rare look out of Rapunzel's window, her eyes narrow, and a small smile cutting into her full cheeks.

'Did you speak to him?'

'Conrad?' Rapunzel's skin burned as she tried to keep her tone normal. 'Yes, he has a request and—'

'Not him. I heard what *he* said and we shall of course weave his blanket, and you will give him one of those gold coins back. Not him, but the young, fine-looking one. Did you speak to him?'

'Of course not,' Rapunzel answered, using her shock at her aunt's generosity towards Conrad to cover her own flush at the mention of the handsome stranger. 'Why would I speak to him? We have no need of him.'

Aunt Gretel studied Rapunzel so intensely the girl was sure she could see right under her skin to the racing, red heart caged beneath. 'Perhaps not. But we could have fun with him,' Aunt Gretel said finally, and then clicked her fingers three times, the sound unnaturally loud, like tiny thunder claps, and flashes of blue appeared from her fingertips.

Something shifted in the tower. Rapunzel felt it

immediately, the air thickening around her, becoming almost tangible, and it was filled with the scents and spirits of the depths of the rivers and oceans and every life the water had ever held. It squeezed her ribs tight and then all was back to normal. Except it wasn't. The air might be forest fresh again, but something had definitely changed. She gripped her workbench to steady herself, her balance lost.

'There,' Aunt Gretel said, satisfied. 'That'll do it.'

'Do what?' Rapunzel looked up, worried.

'I've made it true, of course.' Gretel bustled towards the doorway. 'Your delightful story of having a curse placed on you by a wicked witch. That young man will be back, I would bet my long life on it. He has royal blood, I could smell it on the breeze. Royals always think they're better than all the rest when they are simply, in the main, spoiled and entitled. Men are awful. Royal men are the worst of them. But let's see if he'll take a spindle test in return for a night or two with you outside the tower, my dear.' She patted Rapunzel's cheek affectionately. 'But for now get to work unravelling that blanket and looking at dyes. I think a rainbow pattern would be nice. I shall start on the magic.' She took the two tarts Rapunzel was carrying and smiled, happy. 'Raspberry. Delicious.' And then she was gone, disappearing back to her library.

Rapunzel stared after her in disbelief. Aunt Gretel was joking. Surely she was joking. *Wasn't* she? There was only one way to find out. She kicked her shoes off and ran as fast as she could all the way back down the tower. As she reached the final steps, she slowed, not by choice but because suddenly she felt heavier and as if she was walking through treacle.

Once she reached the hallway, she could barely move at all but she was a strong young woman and so she pushed on, forcing herself towards the door, leaning in against the pressure. When she reached the smooth stone, and whispered the command for the door to appear, the wall remained silent and unchanged.

'Open Sesame.' She said it again, louder this time, or at least as loud as the intense pressure would allow, but still the wall remained just a wall. She moved backwards, the weight on her easing with every step and she was forced to accept the truth. She was trapped inside the tower. She couldn't leave.

Her heart sank as she trudged back up to her workroom. Perhaps it was a bit of fun for Aunt Gretel, but it didn't feel so funny to her. How long would this curse last? Until the nobleman – prince, or even *king*, if Aunt Gretel's comment on his blood was to be believed – had left? Had refused the challenge? From nowhere, tears pricked in the corners of her eyes and her throat ached with the threat of them. She'd had no reason to cry for a very long time and this sudden rush of emotion brought back a hazy memory of sobbing into her pillow, her room, so familiar now, then alien and frightening.

She'd cried out for the man in the crimson jacket – 'Come back, Father' – all through the night, with Aunt Gretel – *a stranger, she was a stranger* – trying to soothe her and failing until sparks came from the old woman's fingers and suddenly Rapunzel felt better. The man in the crimson jacket became the echo of a dream, as did all life before the tower.

For a second, as tears threatened her now, it all almost came back to her, and then her head throbbed and it was gone again like dandelion pollen on the wind.

Her current sadness, however, remained. Despite her trust in Aunt Gretel that all men were cruel or foolish or a terrible combination of both, the stranger had made her blood pound all through her body and she hated the thought she might never see him again. There was no way he'd accept Aunt Gretel's challenge. And even if he did, the odds were against anything good happening to him if he pricked himself on one of their spindles. People very rarely wanted magical items to gift something good to someone.

She needed to put him out of her mind, she decided, as she picked up the blanket and started to unravel the yarn, otherwise she'd go quite mad.

That was, as she thought again of his dark hair and freshwater blue eyes, easier said than done.

Ten

Once he'd eaten a hearty late lunch of Conrad's rich rabbit stew and his host had dozed off in his armchair in front of the fire, the young king quietly left the cabin. He followed the trail of small pebbles Aladdin had left for him until he reached the boy's camp under the heavy boughs of a willow tree by the stream and not far at all from the white tower.

Aladdin was munching on some hard bread from their provisions and looked as if he'd just woken up, his hair askew and eyes bleary, the young king's own dagger glinting at his side. It was strange to see it on the boy, but he could hardly have left him defenceless in the forest. Aladdin yawned and grinned, a definite haze about him. There had been some dwarf beer in the backpack and it seemed likely that Aladdin had availed himself of a draft or two of it while the young king had been away.

'It is as the washerwoman told us,' the king said, smiling as he sat on an old tree trunk. 'Conrad, who lives in the cabin at the edge of the village, *does* take them their provisions. He has taken me in as a guest and I've already been to the tower and seen the girl the witch keeps there. You were right. She is quite beautiful. She has golden hair and pale skin and she barely even glanced my way. She's so different to the women I've met on the road. I will go back tonight and—'

'No, you won't,' Aladdin cut in, and the young king stopped speaking. He knew he should reprimand Aladdin for interrupting him – he was the social superior after all – but there was something about the boy that commanded some respect. And, if the young king thought about it hard, perhaps even a little fear. 'Let *me* go tonight,' Aladdin continued. 'You know nothing about her other than she is beautiful and that is really less than nothing because beauty is a luck of birth. If she's awake and at her window, I'll talk to her. Find out what she likes. Who she is. *Then* you can woo her.'

'But I have to see her again. I must. I cannot lie to you, Aladdin, she took my breath away. I was expecting a challenge, but this is something more.

Perhaps even the promise of love. What if she forgets me between now and then?'

'Trust me,' Aladdin said with a chuckle. 'Nothing dampens a woman's ardour more than an over-eager suitor. If you don't visit tonight, she will want to see you all the more tomorrow.'

'A whole night and day feels so very long.' The young king pulled the remaining dwarf beer from a saddle bag and took an unhappy sip. 'Perhaps you will fall in love with her yourself and understand how I feel.'

Aladdin laughed out loud, a wry mirth, and he shook his young head. 'No fear of that, my friend, no fear of that.'

'You can't be sure,' the young king smiled, remembering his own youth. 'You're of the age for your first infatuation.'

'I have never understood love,' the boy said with a shrug. 'As with most emotions, I'm an observer rather than a participant. So no, I will not find myself her slave as you do.'

He laughed aloud and the young king joined in, but deep in the pit of his gut, where even pampered young kings have a place from which warning signals come, he wished that he hadn't given the boy his dagger. For the first time, he saw beyond the clothes that had lulled him so easily into trust and saw a strange and wily not-quite-adult who was alien to him. Perhaps this final leg of his voyage without his cousin, the duke, was teaching him lessons that a king would need after all.

They chatted a little more, and then the young king returned through the forest to Conrad's cabin, and was relieved to pass a second, more hidden, camp, where one of his six soldiers nodded at him from beside a small fire as he went by. It was ridiculous to be afraid of a mere boy, he told himself. And yet, still, his gut told him to be careful.

He gathered some fallen branches as he walked the last of the pebble trail until the pretty cabin surrounded by plants and flowers and beehives came into view, and he vented his frustration at not seeing the beautiful girl in the tower and at his nervousness about Aladdin chopping them into a neat stack before Conrad woke up.

Eleven

Unlike Aunt Gretel, who'd drunk quite a lot of wine and who Rapunzel could hear snoring loud and contentedly despite the walls and staircase separating their bedrooms, Rapunzel could not sleep. She couldn't even look at the colourful book again because now, whenever she read about the prince, all she could picture was the handsome nobleman and that made her heart quicken and her blood heat and left her in an even worse state.

It was a hot night and she paced her room in the moonlight, constantly checking the window to see if he'd come to her. At least she could lean out of that even if she couldn't open the door downstairs.

How foolish she'd been to share the lie she'd told the boorish travellers with Aunt Gretel. She'd known it would please her but she hadn't thought the ramifications through at all. And what if she never lifted the curse? What if Rapunzel really *was* trapped here for ever waiting for a foolish man to free her? It dawned on her that while she'd never wanted to leave the tower, she had liked knowing she'd had a choice.

She sighed and flopped on her bed. Her skin was tingling so much she thought it might dance right off her flesh and her stomach was filled with jumping beans. Was this the love the book spoke of so much? She'd had to force her supper down though she had no appetite at all, and the long evening of study and chat with Aunt Gretel had been endlessly tedious. All she wanted to do was think about or talk about the handsome stranger, and she could do neither of those things with her aunt.

She couldn't say that perhaps this man was different, not like her own father who abandoned her, or the leering brutish oafs who found their way to her window, or the men in Aunt Gretel's past. She didn't want to worry Aunt Gretel into strengthening the curse so much that maybe even her window would be blocked up, or worse, and she didn't want to upset her. She loved Aunt Gretel with all her heart and she wanted her to be happy.

But still, even as she'd worked, carefully dying the strands of fibre ready to be reborn into a beautiful rainbow blanket, in her mind she was seeing the man's face and imagining his lips on hers and his hands on her body.

Part of her golden hair had come free of its bindings, perhaps from the heat of her thoughts, and the plait trailed to the floor. She was glad it wasn't showing its full length, which would trail down the tower if she hung it all out of her window while free of its magical constraints. She didn't want to be reminded of the disappointments of men. She was too filled with desire.

This was a terrible mess she'd made for herself, she decided with a sigh. Maybe it would be better if the young man didn't come at all. Maybe then all these strange feelings would fade and life could go back to normal. Even as she very firmly thought it, she knew it was a lie. There was nothing she wanted *less* than for the stranger to stay away, despite this constant unbearable ache inside her.

Suddenly, in the quiet of the night, she heard the crunching of twigs, the sound of someone approaching the tower. She leapt to her feet, her breath caught in her throat and rushed to the window to peer out.

'Hello?' she called. 'Is someone down there?'

A young face peered out from behind a tree and looked up at her with impish delight, white teeth shining in the moonlight as he grinned.

'I am Aladdin. At your service.' The boy bowed, deep and low and over-dramatic.

Rapunzel was amused but her heart sank. This definitely wasn't her young nobleman. He wasn't even a fully-grown man yet. Still, she thought, as he came out the shadows and held his lamp up, he was a man in the making and since he wasn't *her* young man she'd carry on as normal, and see how easy it was to play with him. How old was he, she wondered. He looked young, but there was a confidence about him that made her rethink. He wasn't a child. Perhaps thirteen or even a year or two more? An age to think himself grown even if he wasn't.

She leaned forward and smiled back, flirtatiously. 'You are most charming, Aladdin. And handsome, too. How lucky I am you passed this way.'

The boy on the grass below burst into laughter. 'You're very beautiful, but that stuff doesn't work on me.'

'Oh.' She stiffened, momentarily insulted. Normally the young ones – and the old – were the most easily flattered. At the very least she was used to courteousness and curiosity from passers-by. 'Well, then.'

'Do not be offended, fair maiden,' Aladdin said. 'The fault is with me not you. I think, perhaps, I'm not like other people. But I'm also very happy that way. Other people are all so caught up with their own emotions they can rarely see the truth of someone. I don't seem to have that about me. The effect you seek to have on me just won't work.'

He shrugged and laughed again, and something in the laugh brought fragments of a memory back to her. A girl – a friend – with a happy laugh, content with who she was. Dark hair with a single white stripe either side of her face. Or were the colours the other way around? Like the kitten the girl had, with the black and white markings. Her head began to throb and the memories evaporated until she couldn't remember what she'd been remembering, but she decided she liked this boy.

'I'm happy to sit and talk while I eat though, if you want some company?' he said, and promptly sat cross-legged on the ground. 'And we can just be ourselves.'

At first Rapunzel wasn't sure how to answer that but it dawned on her that she was only ever herself with Aunt Gretel and even then, she was so eager to keep her aunt happy, perhaps she didn't quite know who 'herself' really was. Especially after reading the book and seeing the handsome nobleman. A whole new part of her was coming alive, and that part was not going to let her sleep so she may as well have this diversion.

'Very well.' She perched on the thick windowsill. 'So where are you from, Aladdin? And how did you come to be at my tower?' Despite the height from the ground, even when she spoke softly she could be heard and also could hear whoever was below without straining. She supposed that whatever magic held the tower together was designed to make Aunt Gretel's life easier, and, whatever flaws Aunt Gretel had, she wasn't a shouter.

'I'm from the Port of Sinbad in the Kingdom of the Eastern Seas. My father was the most popular spice merchant in the many markets there, well-loved by all, and a master of his trade. He taught me everything he knew, but sadly he and my mother were brutally murdered a year ago, and since then I have had to use my wits to fend for myself.'

'How awful,' she said. 'I have no memory of my own mother or father. I think perhaps my mother died when I was small, and my father . . . all I remember of him is that he wore a crimson jacket.'

'You're saved the grief,' the boy said with a smile. 'Think of it that way.'

'I suppose. You must have been very upset.'

'I was too busy surviving. I have been on pirate ships. I have dived in the Meridien Seas. I wrestled a dwarf once.'

'Tell me.' Rapunzel's eyes widened. 'Tell me all of it.'

And Aladdin did, and she laughed and asked questions, and in her head all the places that seemed so dry in the books she'd read suddenly came alive. In turn, she told him of the men who were all so predictable and how she'd come from somewhere else she couldn't remember, and for the first time in all her years in the tower, she felt like she was making a friend.

Yes, Aladdin was much younger than her, but there was something adult in his ways and perhaps they grew up faster in the Eastern Seas. He'd experienced so much more than she had, and that gave her a pang of sadness. Until tonight she'd thought the outside world only held disappointment and danger, but now she realised that perhaps there was excitement and colour and laughter as well as the danger. And from the stories Aladdin told of jumping free of pirate ships and stealing jewels while people slept, there could be an enormous amount of fun in danger. Maybe – and the thought felt like sacrilege – Aunt Gretel had got some things wrong. After all, she'd been locked away far longer than Rapunzel. Maybe in those long years the kingdoms had changed.

'And what has brought you to the forest, so far away from the seas?' she asked, yawning, as night started once more to turn to day.

'I'm accompanying a young king back to his kingdom,' he said. 'I wanted to expand my horizons, and he needed a companion on his journey. He's staying with a man in the village but I wanted to sleep under the green blanket of the forest canopy, and smell the earth and leaves, so different from the sea and sand.'

Suddenly, Rapunzel was wide awake. 'Does your young king have dark hair and blue eyes?' she asked, as nonchalantly as possible, while her heart hammered in her chest. How many strangers could be in the village at once? And a young king? This was even *more* like the book than if he were just a noble man. 'I think I saw him today. He came with Conrad, who fetches things from the village for us.'

Aladdin's eyes widened. 'So *you* must be the girl he said he'd seen.'

'What exactly did he say?' She leaned out as far as she could, and wished she could run downstairs and get Aladdin to take her to him.

'Well, not a lot.' Aladdin shrugged. 'He didn't mention the tower or anything. He came by to check I was settled in my camp and I asked how his day had been because he wanted to learn about how ordinary people lived, and he said he'd been helping his host with some chores and that he'd seen a pretty girl. That was it.'

'Just pretty? Not beautiful? Most people call me beautiful.'

'I can only tell you what he said.' He paused. 'Maybe it wasn't even you he meant? Maybe it was a girl from the village.' Aladdin yawned and got to his feet. 'Although I do get the feeling he's looking to fall in love.' He yawned again, his mouth stretching wide, and as put out as Rapunzel felt by the apparent lack of instant adoration from the object of her desire, the yawn was catching and she realised she was exhausted too. 'It's been lovely meeting you, Rapunzel. But I have to sleep,' the boy said. 'I'm not sure how long His Highness wants to stay. He said a few days, but royalty have a habit of getting bored quickly. Let's hope he stays longer. I would like us to meet again.' He looked back at her. 'Or of course, perhaps . . .' his words trailed off but there had been the hint of excitement in them, the hint of some kind of plan.

'Perhaps what?' Rapunzel asked, alert.

'Well, maybe I could send the young king in my place to keep you company tomorrow night? I could say that we'd agreed to meet, but then feign some illness and ask him if he'd deliver my apologies to you.'

'Why would you do that?'

'Because, dear sweet Rapunzel,' he grinned up at her, amused, 'I think a handsome young king and a beautiful girl in a tower might make a very good match. Don't you?'

Rapunzel laughed then, a kind and good-natured sound, because at heart she was a kind and good-natured girl, and she knew he'd seen through her.

'Yes, I do. So, it's a plan, my new friend.'

The boy bowed again, deep and low, and then, with them both laughing, he vanished into the forest.

Rapunzel flopped on her bed, her aunt's snores still loud across the stairway, and giggled, her heart leaping. Life in the tower was suddenly a lot more interesting. She'd made a friend and the very next night she'd see her handsome stranger again. And he wasn't a nobleman. He was a young *king*.

It was going to turn out just like the book, she thought, as she sighed happily.

She knew it.

Twelve

It was amazing how little sleep she needed when her heart was fluttering and her feet couldn't stay still. She had Aunt Gretel's breakfast ready for her – a pile of sweet pancakes and some of Conrad's strawberries on top – by the time the sun was creeping through the branches of the trees. As the birds sang merrily outside, Rapunzel couldn't stop smiling. She agreed with the birds. It was a bright, new, wonderful summer's day and they should all be happy. She wanted to dance through the tower and thought she might have to run up and down the stairs a few times like she had when she was younger, just to be able to settle at her work.

She was going to see the young king tonight and he had called her pretty. After much consideration, she'd decided she quite liked that he hadn't gushed about her beauty. She didn't want a man who fawned all over her. How could she respect that? Once they were properly in love, then he would call her beautiful, she was sure of it. And he would look at her and she would see that he loved her without him having to say a word.

As Aunt Gretel always said, words in and of themselves were nothing. It was what sat behind them that gave them power. Love, hate, dishonesty, greed, truth and lies. Words were tools for every human desire. A clever person would always look beyond the words. Rapunzel hoped that when she and the young king met then – like in the book – words wouldn't be needed at all to talk about love. It would just *be*. She wanted his words to make her laugh, and to teach her about all the different places in the world. And then she would teach him everything she'd learned in the tower, of plants and flowers and their uses. Perhaps she would even be able to help the learned healers of his city because she doubted anyone could know as much as Aunt Gretel about these matters.

'Oh, you're a good girl,' Aunt Gretel said, and kissed her on the cheek as she sat at the table and looked through the kitchen window to the beautiful day beyond, ready for her breakfast. 'And up so early.'

'The birds were singing. I caught their enthusiasm for the day.' She smiled and knew she was glowing as hard and hot as the sun outside. 'You sit and relax. I'll get on.'

While Aunt Gretel ate her pancakes and drank her nettle tea in the kitchen, Rapunzel took herself to her room to start work. She was eager to get back to the pretty blanket but also had a spinning wheel to finish smoothing and polishing, and if she got that out of her way, there would be room to dance and twirl and imagine herself at a ball without Aunt Gretel wondering what on earth had got into her.

She spent an hour or so sanding down the surfaces and then rubbing oil into them, so that each part would move smoothly, and paid particular attention to making sure the spindle was honed to a fine point, for while some of the spinning wheels would carry the charm, mainly the magic was in the spindle. When she was done, she carried the spinning wheel carefully up to the large room near Aunt Gretel's library.

As she opened the door, the candles in the sconces lit themselves, as was the way with all the rooms in the magical tower, and she carefully stepped inside. It had been a relatively quiet year for visitors asking for curses and charms and spells, and the room was quite full. In the far corner – where she was taking this particular wheel – there were five or six as yet uncharmed pieces, where the wood was still just wood, and while they would undoubtedly work for spinning, there was no magic in them yet.

Once she'd placed it down, she picked her way back through the full room, where there were perhaps twenty more of different sizes and made from different types of wood, and attached to each was a small piece of parchment, and carefully written in green ink, in her aunt's spidery writing, was a short list of ingredients. None said what the actual curse – most likely – or charm – more rarely – was, only what had gone into making it, as if the ingredients spoke for themselves. And maybe they did. Rapunzel had never really paid that much attention when her aunt tried to explain the components of various spells to her. It wasn't as if she was ever going to have magic of her own. The best she could hope for was to be a magician until whatever items her aunt had left were gone, and given how long witches lived it was highly unlikely Aunt Gretel would die before her anyway. And did she even want to live in the tower all her life anymore? After hearing Aladdin's stories of adventure and thinking of her handsome stranger and his kingdom far away, she wasn't so sure.

She was coming to realise she was very young to

have decided never to live anywhere else. But could she leave Aunt Gretel? Of course she could, she thought as she went back to her own room and sat down to finish weaving Conrad's blanket. She could come back and visit. Or maybe she and the young king could persuade Aunt Gretel to come and live with them in his kingdom. She'd be safe there, and if she wanted her own space, she could probably build herself a magic kingdom in the castle grounds. It could all work out very nicely indeed and maybe they'd all live happily ever after.

She lost herself in imaginings of castle life as the wool shifted beneath her fingers, and before she knew it, two hours had passed and the blanket was finished. Her back ached and her fingers were sore but she was pleased with how beautiful the rainbow colours looked and knew that even without the magic Aunt Gretel would add it would make the child and his family happy. Perhaps she would have a child of her own with the young king one day, she thought, as she stretched out her tight muscles and then went to find her aunt. How lovely would that be?

'I've finished it,' she said, smiling with pride as she handed it over. 'What do you think?'

'You've done very well, dear.' Aunt Gretel nodded approvingly. 'Fine work indeed. And now shall we add the final touches?' She winked, her eyes twinkling in her round face, and Rapunzel had a rush of loving her aunt very much. She was, after all, the only family she could remember.

As Rapunzel held the blanket open, Aunt Gretel pulled two vials from her cupboard – one of water from deep in the deepest pond beneath the old willow tree villages over, and another filled with a thick deep red liquid that almost glittered – Aunt Gretel's own blood. First, she used the pond water, shaking a few drops across the wool, and then, with more care, she removed the dropper from the vial of blood.

'And what are the rules with a witch's blood?' she asked as she held the dropper over the brightest pink strip of wool.

'One drop for the gentlest touch, two for strong magic, but three is always too much.'

'Correct.' Aunt Gretel smiled and then let one drop fall from the dropper to the blanket. After a moment, as if an afterthought, she released a second. 'There. That will do it.'

As she turned to replace the vials, Rapunzel was once again surprised at her Aunt's generosity. First, she was only charging Conrad one gold coin for the charmed blanket, and now she was being generous with the magic itself. It wasn't as if it was an easy thing to do. Extracting a witch's blood was a painful process and each drop was a part of their life gone. For someone who was so quick to call Conrad a fool and a simpleton, it was clear Aunt Gretel thought fondly of him.

'Right,' her aunt said, satisfied. 'Now we let it set until tomorrow. I think we've earned a good lunch. Is there any of that pink sponge cake left? Or maybe the last of those jam tarts.'

Thirteen

It had been a hot day and the night had cooled just enough for the warmth to be pleasant, even for Aladdin, who was used to the shimmering heat of the desert and salty seas. He was feeling very pleased with himself as he led the young king through the forest towards the white tower. What he lacked in human emotion, he more than made up for in brains. One evening chatting to the maiden in the tower and he knew everything he needed to know about her to get what he wanted. Soon he would have all the witch's spinning wheels and then once he was back in Sinbad, his dreams of power and wealth would come true.

Beside him, the young king was droning on about the great beauty of the girl, *as dazzling as a child of sun and stars* – somewhat of an exaggeration, if Aladdin was being honest, but then he was learning that the king was prone to grandiose statements – and as they drew closer to the tower, he brought his attention back to his companion.

'I don't think that kind of flattery will work on Rapunzel,' he said quietly. 'I learned a lot about her last night, and while she is all the things you could wish for – a maiden, fair and unspoilt, who will no doubt be exceptionally grateful when you free her from that tower – flattery will not woo her.'

'Are you saying I should insult her?' The young king was puzzled, and Aladdin sighed. How was it he could be so young and yet understand so much more than this man?

'Of course not. That has never worked for a woman either, trust me. No, I think Rapunzel is looking for someone who *sees* her. And you need to be witty. Charming. Confident. She must know you think she's beautiful, but don't over-praise her. Let her be intrigued by you.'

'It sounds like a lot of hard work,' the young king said. 'Can't I just recite her some sonnets? I know plenty by heart and if I switch a few words around she'll think they're just for her.'

'You wanted a challenge,' Aladdin said. 'You've had easy wenches in Sinbad and no doubt half the villages between here and your own Kingdom of the High Born. Maybe you'll even fall in love with this one.'

'She *is* very beautiful,' the young king said wistfully. 'And her skin is pale as moonlight itself. How I long to touch it.' Aladdin took a long hard look at him. While Rapunzel might be dazzled by his title and good looks, those would wear off fast if he couldn't make her laugh and dazzle her as much with his personality. And if that happened, he had no chance of his plan working. Rapunzel had to *want* the young king as much as he did her.

As they approached the final cluster of trees nearest the tower that shone like a lighthouse under the bright full moon, he had an idea, a change from their original plan of Aladdin simply listening and watching out for any passers-by.

'You need to let me do the talking,' he said, softly, holding the king back from venturing forward into the open clearing and the pool of moonlight, ready to place him centre stage under Rapunzel's gaze.

'What do you mean?'

'I know her better than you. I can give you the right words to say to make her want you.'

'Of course she'll want me,' the young king said. 'All the girls always do.'

'She is not all girls, Your Highness. And I promise I can deliver her to you. Of course,' he added, smoothly, 'it will be you she falls in love with properly. Once she's in your arms. You just need my help to get her there.'

'So, what do you suggest? I thought you'd led her to believe we'd be alone.'

'And you will. But if you don't go too far forward, then I can hide in that copse there . . .' He pointed to a small cluster of young trees closer to the tower than the rest. 'And then I can whisper suggestions to you if I think you need them. How to react. The occasional joke. Perhaps help with the plan to free her from her aunt?'

The young king nodded, thoughtful. 'Like an advisor,' he said. 'My father was a great believer in surrounding oneself with good advisors.'

'Just like that,' Aladdin said with a smile. He paused then, and looked up. Golden hair glinted bright under the stars. 'She's waiting.'

As the young king stepped forward, Aladdin, with all the wiles his tricky life had bestowed upon him and knowing that in these first few seconds Rapunzel would have eyes only for the young man, darted unnoticed into the copse.

The king did as he was told and didn't walk too far ahead. He was about to go into a deep bow when

Aladdin hissed a quick, 'No! Be casual!' and the king managed to turn the movement into the removal of his cape. Aladdin was happy with that. It showed off his thick arms and strong chest.

Aladdin sat cross-legged on the soft long grass beneath the tree, and the gentle breeze that rustled through the branches above ceased almost immediately, as if even nature wanted to help him with his plan. Both young voices carried to him where he sat, and as Rapunzel leaned out of her window, smiling, he knew this would be easy. She *wanted* to fall in love with this young king and the young king wanted to think he'd fallen in love with her in return, so they would see past the flaws in each other to make it true – for a while, at least.

After his initial awkwardness, the young king stretched out casually across the grass on his side, legs crossed and propped up on one elbow, and his grin was easy and charming. He did not call Rapunzel beautiful but kept with 'pretty' and, as she quizzed him on his life and kingdom, she didn't seem to notice the small pauses that came before her suitor responded. The young king, in turn, did as he was told and barely uttered a word that came from his own mind, instead repeating, parrot fashion, whatever Aladdin whispered to him.

Within half an hour Rapunzel was sipping wine on her window ledge and the young king was sipping wine from his gourd and they were both laughing and chatting as naturally as any young couple wooing each other could be. Only as night began to shift once more towards day did the young woman let out a wistful sigh. 'Oh, how I would like to be able to stand close to you. Maybe dance. I should have taken the opportunity when you came with Conrad, before my aunt realised a handsome young king had visited and sealed up the door to me.'

'I love dancing as much as any other nobleman,' the young king replied with Aladdin's words. 'But trust me, if you were down here it would be a kiss I was after, not a waltz.'

'You're very confident that I'd allow that,' she said.

'Yes, I am.' The young king grinned and winked. 'You did just call me handsome, after all.'

His cockiness made her laugh some more, but then, as he got to his feet, he added, 'But lovely as you are I'd rather have the kiss without an ardour-dampening threat of death by spindle beforehand.'

'So, you don't wish to spend any more time with me?' Rapunzel's laughter vanished, and her surprise and hurt was clear in her tone.

'Oh, I do,' the young king countered. 'Trust me, I

really do. And I will. But this is going to take some planning.' He whipped his cloak around his shoulders and smiled up at her. 'And thankfully, I've had an idea.'

Fourteen

Rapunzel hadn't slept a wink and didn't think she'd ever need to sleep again. She was too giddy with happiness and excitement. When she'd said a very reluctant farewell to the young king she'd stretched out on the bed and let the morning breeze caress her body, her own fingers joining in, and she'd imagined the king doing all the things done in the book – even the things that had made her blush with shock when reading them – to her and she to him. In fact, she imagined it all twice. He was so handsome and witty and charming that he totally dazzled her. He was clever too, and that was what she liked best about him as well as his easy grin, and his blue eyes and that thick black hair she wanted to run her fingers through. She sighed. She liked everything about him. Absolutely everything. He was perfectly perfect and she was the luckiest girl in the world that he seemed to think she was perfect too.

As she watched her aunt fussing around the kitchen, smearing thick honey on buttered bread for her breakfast, she did feel a pang of guilt that she and her young king were plotting to trick Gretel. It had always been her and Aunt Gretel against the world of men, and here she was conspiring with the biological enemy. But no one had told her that a man could make her feel so good, and maybe once Aunt Gretel saw how in love she and the king truly were, then she'd understand. It wasn't as if he was some travelling salesman, she reasoned to herself. He was a king. She'd live in a castle – maybe not so different to living in the tower just a lot bigger – and people would look after her and she'd have beautiful children and she'd never want for anything. How could Aunt Gretel not be happy with that?

But still, she couldn't quite shake off the slippery, unpleasant feeling that she was betraying her aunt. Deceiving her. Because, if she was so sure that Aunt Gretel would be happy for her, why wasn't she just being honest and telling her she wanted to spend time with the young king?

Part of it, she decided, as she went to her room and

looked out of the window, was the excitement of it all. The secrecy of the young king's plan. For the first time in her life – or at least what she could remember of it – Rapunzel felt rebellious, and that was delicious. It made her feel alive. Anyway, she thought, as Conrad's horse snorted and his cart came into view, no one was going to get hurt. And her aunt would never know what they'd done. She'd get time with her young king and then freedom, and her aunt would think it was all fate and accept it. They'd all be happier in the castle in the long run. She was sure of it.

'Conrad's here,' she went back to the hallway and called across to Aunt Gretel.

'Well, go on then.' Her aunt appeared, looking at her expectantly. 'You know what we need. The usual. And more of those iced banana breads. They were delicious.'

'I would if I could,' Rapunzel countered. 'But I can't open the door anymore and it's like walking into a gale just trying to get near it. The curse, remember?' She paused. 'Unless of course you want to lift it for now.'

'A curse is a curse. You can't just lift and lower them whenever you want.' She shook her head, as if Rapunzel should have known that, and maybe, if she'd paid more attention to her books, she would have. 'If I lift it then it's much harder to lower it again, irritating as that is. I'll have to go down myself.'

'Well, hopefully when this joke is over you'll lift the curse for good.'

'Of course I will, darling girl.' Aunt Gretel looked at her with affection and smiled as Rapunzel handed over the rainbow blanket. 'Once this young man, who seems so stunned by you, has shown his true colours and we've had our fun laughing at him.' She handed Rapunzel her slice of bread and honey and adjusted her outfit over her portly figure, before wiping breadcrumbs from her chin. Rapunzel couldn't imagine ever laughing at the young king or thinking him anything other than perfectly amazing, but she smiled back in agreement.

'Oh, and Aunt Gretel,' Rapunzel called down, almost as an afterthought, as the older woman huffed and puffed her way down the stairs. 'I want to make a cradle for the baby. As a gift. From me.'

Aunt Gretel turned and looked at her, surprised but not displeased. 'That's very kind of you.'

'I want to practice my woodworking on something other than spinning wheels. A cradle seems a good enough challenge.'

Gretel nodded. 'A cradle carries magic well. New life is potent. So much innocence. It will do no harm for you to know how to make one.'

'I'll need a basket of wood brought to me tomorrow. Tell Conrad. All different kinds so I can experiment. Large solid pieces. He can load the pulley for you, I'm sure. Tell him, won't you?'

'Of course I'll tell him!' Aunt Gretel said. 'I'm hardly going to forget between here and the door!'

Rapunzel watched, pleased, as her aunt hurried down the stairs, despite always telling Rapunzel to take her time and be aloof. She was absently tucking strands of her hair behind her ears and smoothing down her clothes. Not that Rapunzel was giving her aunt a lot of thought. Her heart was racing too madly. She'd made the first move. The plan was in action. Now it was down to the young king to do his part.

Fifteen

When the door appeared and Gretel was there in front of him instead of Rapunzel, Conrad was so surprised that his face flushed bright red and he stumbled back a couple of paces on his bow legs that he wished had at least once been long and strong like the young king's rather than forever making his walk a waddle. He wondered if the beautiful ever realised what life was like for those born plain, how they might all share the same sun but everything in life was so very different when you were always in the shade.

'Don't look so terrified,' Gretel huffed. 'I'm allowed to answer my own door sometimes.' She held out the small list of items they needed that normally her young ward would give him.

'I'm not terrified,' Conrad chortled. The very

thought made him smile. She didn't know it but he wasn't sure if any of the villagers were scared of Gretel anymore. Maybe at first, before they understood, but not anymore. Perhaps one day she'd realise that wasn't such a bad thing and finally come out and join the world. 'I'm pleasantly surprised. And here.' In return for the note he gave her a small bundle wrapped in a napkin. 'Some sweet cakes and currant buns from my sister and her husband. They know you like the iced ones best.'

'You look tired.' Gretel's eyes narrowed as he stepped closer. 'Everything all right?'

'The baby has a little fever. A cough.' He tried to keep his tone light with a shrug. 'I'm sure it will be fine. They do worry you though, don't they? So small and fragile.'

'I wouldn't know anything about that. Babies and I have never had much to do with each other.'

Once again Conrad saw her defences toughen. Had she – like him – perhaps once yearned for a baby of her own? She had Rapunzel but he knew – even if he struggled to remember – that the young woman had not been here as a small child let alone an infant. Maybe in a time before the tower, when Gretel had been different, she'd thought a family might be in her future.

'But I'm sure he'll get better.' Gretel held out the blanket and in the bright sunlight the stripes of colour glittered and shone. 'This should help.'

'Oh, it's beautiful.' Tears sprung to the corners of his eyes and he knew just by looking at the reworked wool that the baby would be gurgling happily within hours of being wrapped in it. Even though the magic wasn't meant for him he could feel it on his fingertips and he was sure the niggles in the base of his back from gardening, which reminded him that his youth was pretty much behind him, were easing up already. 'Thank you so much. There's not enough gold in the world to pay you for the relief this will bring.'

'Yes, speaking of which,' Gretel said disdainfully, rummaging with her free hand in the pocket of her dress. 'Take this back.'

Not one but both of his gold coins flashed in her hand and then he felt the weight of them in his own. He looked up at her, confused. 'I don't understand. The blanket . . .'

'Don't worry, the blanket has plenty of magic in it. But I don't need your gold. Judging from your clothes, donkey and cart, the money could be better spent elsewhere.'

'I don't know what to say.' Once again tears threatened to come, Conrad being an openly emotional man and not used to such generosity in life. 'How can I thank you?'

'Thanks are unnecessary. But tell a soul of this and I'll turn you into a maggot.'

Conrad nodded, carefully tucking the coins away for safekeeping, and turning back to go to his cart.

'I'll walk with you,' Gretel said and stepped across the threshold. 'I want to check my flowers and herb gardens. There were slugs last year. Very persistent ones.'

Conrad couldn't believe that any slug or snail had ever invaded the beautiful moat of flowers and plant life that surrounded Gretel's tower, and as they strolled back towards where the young king was waiting on the narrow track with the cart, he enjoyed the assault of various scents carrying on the fresh morning air.

'These peonies are beautiful,' he said, as they passed a patch of bright blooms that were all shades of purple and pinks.

'My favourite.' She looked at them with something close to a warm affection. 'They were already growing here before I came. I saw them and knew I would be . . .' She stopped herself there, and stiffened slightly. 'Oh, and Rapunzel needs some wood. A lot of it. A variety of types. She's starting a new project. This afternoon?'

Conrad nodded, happy to oblige. Despite his lack of sleep he felt invigorated, and as soon as he'd delivered the blanket he'd have peace of mind about the child and would happily spend hours chopping and gathering wood for Rapunzel if he needed to. He was sure the young king would help too if asked.

The young man in question came into view, looking up from his place at the cart to a fixed point behind them. Conrad didn't need magic to know he was looking at Rapunzel's window. Judging by the pained expression on the lad's face, there was no one looking back.

'It seems like yesterday I was his age,' he said with a smile. 'Everything ahead. Life. The hope of love. Mistakes to be made.' He let out a sigh. 'We all need those things, don't you think, Gretel? To live. To love. To make mistakes and learn from them.' He looked into her eyes and thought they were the palest, most arresting blue he'd ever seen. 'Even you.

'What happened to you was terrible.' For a moment he almost saw beyond the wall she'd put up around herself higher than any tower, to the woman beyond. 'But it was a long—'

'Send the wretched boy with the wood later,' she snapped, her tone as cold as her ice-blue eyes.

'I'm sorry, I didn't mean—'

She turned on her heel and, with her back stiff, strode back towards her tower. Conrad's good mood crumpled in on itself, disappearing to nothing. He should have known better. She'd made him the blanket *and* given him his money back and still he'd pushed too far. In all these years, he'd clearly learned nothing. For reasons he didn't quite understand, her anger at him made him feel almost worse than anything else.

His shoulders slumped, and he was about to let despondency take over, when she called over her shoulder to him.

'I don't want you carrying such a heavy load. I can see your back is giving you trouble.' She still looked hurt, but that rage at him had gone and he couldn't help but grin at her like a teenage fool.

'As you wish, Gretel. But I'm not that old yet.'

He thought he saw just the hint of a smile cross her lips, and that was enough to buoy his mood again. He almost leapt up into the cart with the ease he'd had as a teenager.

He saw the young king's own expression change, and looked up to the window to see that Rapunzel had finally appeared, just as they were leaving. She'd waited until her Aunt Gretel was under the shade of the tower so she wouldn't notice. Conrad looked from her to the young royal beside him and back again, and wasn't sure quite how he felt about the looks that the two were giving each other. He liked the young king, but their short time together was teaching him a lot about how different those of noble birth were to the common folk. He was used to getting his own way in all things, that was clear, and he had a confidence that could only come from a life of privilege.

But still, he thought, as he clicked his tongue to get Daisy, his faithful donkey, moving, Rapunzel was young. She deserved some adventure and romance, even if perhaps it would not be *the* romance. What harm could such things do, after all?

Sixteen

It was late afternoon when the young king returned to the white tower with the large heavy basket on the back of the cart. His shoulders ached from having chopped and gathered more than was required for the task, and on reflection he wished he *had* let his host help him, but this was his plan and it was best that Conrad was kept as far away from it as possible.

His plan. Well, it had come from his mouth and it would certainly have been his plan when he was back home and recounting it to his friends and advisors. His heart thumped, nervously, as he loosely tied Daisy's reins around the thick trunk of an old tree and readied himself to carry the heavy basket to the tower and face the witch.

He was excited by the prospect of what they'd planned but suddenly it all seemed very real. He hadn't even told his six mercenaries what he was doing, but even if he had, he doubted anything to do with witches came under their remit. And what could go wrong really, he asked himself for the hundredth time. The girl was clearly smitten with him, just as he was filled with desire for her. His longing to have her was a constant heat beneath his skin.

Still, he'd had a lot of time to think while chopping wood he didn't need and it was hard not to feel apprehensive. He was the one who was going to be pricked with the spindle after all and, while Aladdin had no doubts about their plan, there was always margin for error, and he'd be the one paying the price for any mistakes.

There would be no mistakes, he told himself firmly, as he lifted the basket down and strode towards the tower, trying not to groan at the weight of it. The girl was in love with him. She'd make sure he chose a good spindle. That was also something to be excited about. Not only would he deflower this beautiful maiden but he'd get an enchantment too. Perhaps it would promise him victory in every battle during his reign. He could go to the Battle Lands himself if that was the case and be assured of coming home safe and covered in glory. The thought of that made his pace quicken as the door to the tower opened and the witch showed herself. An enchantment like that would do very nicely indeed.

In the doorway, the witch looked him up and down and then snorted. 'You look like you're going to burst a blood vessel carrying that load. Should I take it?'

'I would never expect a lady to carry anything when there is a gentleman present.'

'A lady?' she snorted.

While she resembled a few of the nannies who helped raise him in many ways – a thickening waist and full rosy cheeks – her eyes were the coldest blue he'd ever seen and her hair was like the ice on the side of the Far Mountain that had defeated his climb. It wasn't grey with age, she wasn't old enough yet for that, but so pale a blonde it almost shimmered to the edge of blue when the sun hit it. If he was honest, everything about her unnerved him.

'I've never trusted a man with too many manners. So much is just surface vanity. I'm a witch, boy, and you'd best remember it. Your royal blood carries no weight here.'

'I did not mean to offend you,' he said, wondering if he should dump the basket and its contents where he stood, run back to the cart and keep running until he reached home. It was then that a shadow high above caught his attention and he glanced up to see Rapunzel peering down over the edge of the banister at the top of the tower. Even from this distance her beauty took his breath away, and he could hardly behave like a coward and flee right in front of her. He took a deep breath and steadied his nerves.

'Perhaps I could carry the basket upstairs for you? I could take it to Rapunzel.' He made sure he sounded full enough of yearning for the witch to notice.

'Just attach it to the winch,' she said. 'The girl is perfectly capable of pulling it up herself.'

He stepped across the threshold and his arms screamed as he attached the heavy load to the basket and then looked up again, smiling at Rapunzel, who ducked out of view. With the sound of distant cranking, the wood began to slowly rise.

'She is so very beautiful,' he said wistfully, as he returned to the afternoon sunshine outside. 'Perhaps you would allow me to take her to the village for an evening? I would like to get to know her better.'

Gretel's smile grew. 'She can't leave the tower. Certainly not so easily. She's under a curse to protect her from the wiles of men. And there is the risk of a fate worse than death for any man – or royal – who thinks to try to break it.' She looked him up and down as a cat might a cornered mouse. 'But if you're willing to take the risk then the reward will be your heart's desire. Two nights with the beautiful Rapunzel. And if she loves you after that then she is free to leave with you.'

The young king listened, and then asked questions to keep her talking as the witch told him what he already knew. He had to choose from one of her spindles and allow himself to be either cursed or enchanted, with the likelihood to be far more the former than the latter, and with the spell binding to him for life. Whatever he chose, there could be no going back from it, good or bad.

'I am willing to take that chance,' the young king said, while feeling very much *unwilling* to take that chance in the present moment, when her words sounded so full of doom.

'I am not so cruel,' the witch retorted. 'I understand the impetuousness of youth. You have three nights to think over your decision. Return on the fourth evening from now and tell me if you still wish to proceed. And remember – there are more curses than charms in my collection, just as in the world of men.'

The young king stepped back, and then bowed. 'Tell Rapunzel I shall return.'

'And if you do, then you truly are a fool,' Gretel answered, and then the door vanished and he was left bowing to the wall.

Seventeen

As soon as the winch had brought the large basket to the top of the tower, Rapunzel quickly pulled away the top layer of wood so that Aladdin could leap out. Between them, they carried the wood into her room and the boy slid – somewhat reluctantly – under her bed. When Aunt Gretel had been outside talking to Conrad that morning Rapunzel had stashed water, some bread and cheese, and a sweet tart in the boy's hiding space, and now that he was concealed she shoved the basket up against her bed, covering any view of the floor and making a show of examining some of the wood when Aunt Gretel joined her.

'I thought you'd need help with the basket,' she said, surprised. 'The young idiot was struggling with it despite pretending not to be.'

'Then he is weak as well as an idiot,' Rapunzel answered.

'Indeed. But we shan't be seeing him again. So, if you were at all intrigued by his handsome face, I'd get yourself to the window because it's probably the last time you're going to see it.'

'How so?' Rapunzel pretended to seem perplexed.

'It would appear you made quite an impression on him. He asked if he could spend an evening in your company and I told him my terms.' She chortled to herself. 'He said he'll be back three evenings from now. I predict he'll be a hundred miles away by then.'

Rapunzel ambled to the window and idly glanced out, a vision of beautiful disinterest even as her heart threatened to explode from her body when she glimpsed the thick dark curls on the young king's head. 'What if he *does* come back?' she asked. 'What then? Will you hold him to it?'

'I'm a witch,' Gretel said, somewhat put out. 'My word is my bond.'

'So, you'll make him choose one?'

'I won't *make* him do anything, my dear. It will be entirely his own decision.' She smiled and winked at Rapunzel. 'But it will entertain us these few days even though he won't return.'

'Yes,' Rapunzel agreed. 'It will.' She watched as

114

the young king glanced up and smiled at her, so hungrily, and as soon as Aunt Gretel turned away, she smiled back and her heart sang. Three more nights and then she'd be in his arms. And all this would be worth it.

The rest of the afternoon and evening once again passed so slowly, but she had to remind herself that they were worse for Aladdin. She wasn't in the habit of closing her workroom door during the day so the boy had to stay still and quiet while she worked, especially as Aunt Gretel was in such a good mood that she was bustling around the place and baking cakes and buns of her own, bringing samples in for Rapunzel to taste.

Unlike Aunt Gretel, Rapunzel didn't care much for sweet treats, but she dutifully made all the right appreciative noises, and her aunt was pleased. It wasn't just the baking or Rapunzel that was bringing her aunt joy. She'd forgotten how much doing a little magic made the older woman happy. She was only like this when clients came to her with problems that only her magic could solve and she would spend days baking and thinking and pondering and eating before the right curse or charm came to her.

Aunt Gretel said that magic and fate were brother and sister, and a witch was merely a vessel for both.

When a problem came along, it was fate that provided the solution, coming in the form of an incomplete dream or a vision, and then the witch had to do the work to make it real.

Rapunzel was often very glad that she was not a witch. Her aunt made light of it but using her magic drained her. These highs of enchantment were followed by deep exhausted lows when the charm was done. Nothing in life was free, Aunt Gretel said, and the rarer the gift the higher the price. She'd been born with the gift of magic and she had paid a high price for it too. Her face would darken then and leave Rapunzel wondering once again what in her life had brought Gretel to the tower.

When dusk had fallen, Rapunzel made a stew for dinner and laced her aunt's portion with a little valerian root. By the time she'd eaten that and drunk a glass of wine, Aunt Gretel was yawning a good few hours before her normal bedtime.

'It's the promise of magic,' Rapunzel said, as they bid each other goodnight and returned to their rooms. 'It's exhausting you. And all the baking.'

'Yes, that must be it. Still, an early night never hurt anyone. You should have one yourself. You look a little tired.'

'I will, Aunt Gretel. I love you.' And even though

she was scheming behind her aunt's back, Rapunzel really did mean it.

As her aunt's door closed, she took a deep breath. It was time to start her part of the plan.

Eighteen

It had to be said, Aladdin was getting fed up of being stuck in dark cramped spaces for long periods of time, first the stinking barrel, and now the narrow gap under Rapunzel's bed, where every speck of sanded wood seemed to have gathered to try to make him sneeze, but at least this time there was some food and water, even if his movement was horribly restricted. He had three more days of hiding to go, by the end of which he knew he was going to be in the foulest of moods, and it was going to take something more than the spindles to return him to good humour. Slaughtering the six mercenaries would go some way towards cheering him up.

It was a relief when, as soon as the first deep snore rumbled through the tower, Rapunzel dragged the wood basket out of the way and he could wriggle free.

'Let's get started,' she said, with a delighted grin, as he stretched and groaned, and moaned about needing a piss. She was actually much prettier when she was like this, not *trying* to be something, and Aladdin decided that, as much as he was capable of liking anyone, he liked Rapunzel. There was something engaging about her, and if she'd seen more of the world, and perhaps had one or two knocks, then she could be a force to be reckoned with.

'Lead the way,' he countered, and as she did, any dregs of bad mood that remained evaporated. Things could not be better in the white tower he concluded as she showed him from room to room and he noted that not a single door or cupboard was locked. First there were the spinning wheels themselves, and his mouth watered as he took note of how many there were, especially when Rapunzel told him it was mainly the spindles that held the charms – of which his quick eye and mind calculated there were twenty-three – which would make it a lot easier to get away with them. Most would fit into his knapsack if he fitted them tightly.

They went around the room, methodically copying down the ingredients of potions on each label into a small notebook and then Rapunzel showed him the library. It was a feast for his eyes. Aladdin knew that information could be as valuable as gold, and this room was a treasure trove of knowledge.

There were books on the science and magic of dragons, and genies, and giants, but Aladdin tossed these to one side, reaching instead for the ones they needed – those focused on spells and the uses of plants and herbs and roots and spices. There was also a large cabinet of curiosities, some of which even Rapunzel couldn't fathom. But what excited him most was the small vial of witch's blood. The true magic that gave power to a charm. He held it up and was sure that it almost glittered through the glass.

'One drop for the gentlest touch, two for strong magic, but three is always too much.' Rapunzel said quietly. 'Aunt Gretel rarely uses more than one, especially in a curse.' She looked at the bottle thoughtfully. 'Perhaps we can add an extra drop to the spindle we decide the king will choose.'

'Perhaps we can,' he agreed, a mischievous smile dancing on his lips, as his mind wandered to all the fun he could have with the witch's blood.

After that, they got down to work, and pored over all the books they could find space to spread around them by candlelight, treating their research methodically, going through the uses for each item and then cross-referencing combinations until their eyes hurt from the strain. At the start, Rapunzel had claimed not to know very much, not having really paid attention to her aunt's lessons, but as time went on more and more came back to her, and Aladdin realised that the same could be said for what his father had taught him about spices. If you were told something over and over, eventually, whether you liked it or not, it went in.

Aladdin fuelled his work by munching on the witch's cakes, biscuits and buns, and Rapunzel had laughed at him, and then wondered if everyone except her had a sweet tooth, and he thought once again what a babe in the woods the young woman was.

If she did choose to leave the tower when this was done, what would she make of the world outside, he wondered. Her beauty and her naivety were surely a combination that would bring her trouble, however sharp her mind. One thing he was sure of, she was never going to be Queen of the Kingdom of the High Born, whatever the young king might tell her. In the moment of asking, the young king himself might believe she would be, but it would never happen.

Still, he thought, bleary-eyed as they finished up their labours for the night and put the books back carefully where they'd found them, that wasn't his problem. He was here for the spindles and after that the genie. That was all.

He hadn't thought that he'd be able to sleep on the hard floor under the bed, even though Rapunzel had given him some of her clothes to use as a pillow and cover, but as soon as his eyes closed, exhaustion claimed him. If he could sleep through the long day, all the better. Two more nights and they'd be done.

Nineteen

Rapunzel thought that the three nights would pass excruciatingly slowly, but in fact she was so busy pretending everything was normal during the days, grabbing a couple of hours sleep where she could, and then working with Aladdin all night, that the hours flew by. She had never studied so hard in her life, but when they finished at the end of the third night, she could have passed any test in magical components Aunt Gretel chose to set.

She had been surprised by how much she already knew and, as they researched each listed item on each spinning wheel, she grew more and more confident about how they combined to create unique charms and curses. There were base ingredients for love, health, wealth, revenge and death, and the additions on top refined each individual item. The addition of a tincture could add lust or make the charm negative or positive, and further ingredients would personalise the charm. It was almost scientific before the witch's blood – the ingredient that made it all work – was added.

When they were done, they stood side by side, the young woman and the wiry boy, and stared at the room of spinning wheels.

'Back row, third from the left,' Rapunzel said, her neck aching. 'That's the one he needs to pick.'

'Are you sure?' Aladdin looked at her, doubtful. 'What about that one at the front? Vanquish your enemy? He might like that.'

'Sounds unpleasant. And whoever the enemy is, they might not have actually done anything wrong. I've read the histories of the Battle Lands. It seems to me a lot of wars are pointless and unnecessary and don't change anything anyway.'

'You may well have a point there. But I just think—'

'No,' she said, firmly. 'Back row, third from the left. The mahogany and elm one. That will do very well indeed.'

They closed the door and crept back down to her bedroom, and by the time they got to the window, the night sky was washed with a pale blue, and the early birds were just starting to sing.

Exhausted as she was, Rapunzel still adjusted her clothing and added a little rouge to her cheeks and lips, much to Aladdin's amusement, before leaning out of the window.

It was her first sight of the young king since he'd snuck Aladdin inside, and her heart leaped and her tiredness was forgotten. He was every bit as handsome as she remembered and maybe even more, and she was sure she glowed as bright as any lamp with the heat he sparked inside her.

'We're ready,' she whispered, excited, and then told him which spindle to choose. She hadn't realised he'd looked nervous until he smiled at her, relieved.

'And what is the charm?'

'It's a surprise. But I think you'll like it.'

'I cannot wait to hold you in my arms tomorrow night, my love. That is all I long for.'

Rapunzel was happy that the days apart hadn't doused his ardour for her, but she was surprised by how earnest he was being. She'd half-expected some irreverent and slightly rude answer to her 'surprise'. Something that would make her laugh rather than something so courtly and from the heart. His words were sweet enough, but not like the man who had entertained her with witty banter when he'd laid on the grass and they'd talked all night. She didn't really have time to think about it, because the heavy rumble of Aunt Gretel's snoring that had kept them company all night suddenly went silent. Aladdin immediately scooted under the bed just in case, and Rapunzel leaned out further.

'You'd better go,' she whispered urgently. 'I think my aunt is waking up.'

The young king didn't hesitate, but blew a kiss up to her, and turned, disappearing quickly into the woods.

Tonight, she thought, as she lay on her bed, staring up at the ceiling. Tonight he would be hers.

***

It was very difficult to keep her face impassive as Aunt Gretel brought the young king into the spinning wheel room. Rapunzel was doing her very best to remain cool and aloof, but when she saw him close up for the first time in what felt like forever, she almost burst with excitement and it took all her control to keep her feet planted where they were. He was dressed in his finest clothes of blue and gold but Aunt Gretel remained decidedly unimpressed.

'Your foolish suitor has arrived,' Aunt Gretel said

with a derisive grunt as the young king stepped further inside the spindle room. His eyes met Rapunzel's and she could see he was nervous, which again, was at odds with what she was expecting. He'd been so devil-may-care that she presumed he'd be finding all this as secretly entertaining as she and Aladdin – who was most annoyed he had to stay under her bed and miss the choosing part – were. The thrill of their caper was fuelling her after so little sleep for days, and she'd expected to see the same humour in his beautiful, blue eyes.

'So I see.' She stood tall, her neck long and her head tilted upwards, proudly. 'So, you've come to choose. Willing to risk everything for two evenings to woo me?'

The young king swallowed, before answering, 'Yes. Yes, I am.'

His adam's apple bobbed once or twice as he swallowed some more, his mouth obviously dry with nerves, and Rapunzel once again had that feeling that something wasn't quite right. A small knot tightened in her stomach, warning her of something, she wasn't sure what, but she pushed it aside, as his hesitant gaze started to wander over the spinning wheels.

He looked exactly the same. He was her young, handsome king. She was tired, that was all. When they were in the forest together later, he'd be her charming, brave suitor once more.

'You can still change your mind,' Aunt Gretel reminded him. 'She's just a girl, and there are plenty of those in the village that come without such a hefty price tag. Don't make a mistake now that you may regret for the rest of your life.'

Was Aunt Gretel nervous, Rapunzel wondered, surprised. She sounded it. That was a surprise too, because Aunt Gretel had nothing but contempt for the opposite sex from paupers to noblemen. Maybe there was still some warmth in her heart for them after all.

'Hurry up and choose,' Rapunzel said, impatiently, as if the whole business was a waste of her time and she cared not a jot about their handsome visitor. 'If you're brave enough. Which perhaps you are not.'

'There are no cowards in the Kingdom of the High Born,' the young king answered, sounding quite put out as if he believed she'd meant what she said, and Aunt Gretel let out a curt laugh.

'If you believe that then you are truly a fool. There are cowards and knaves in every kingdom.'

The young king took a deep breath and his eyes briefly met Rapunzel's own, before he finally spoke. 'That one. At the back. Third from the left. I choose that one.'

For a moment there was silence and Rapunzel realised that she was holding her breath, her heart pounding immediately faster. What if she'd made a mistake? Misunderstood what the ingredients did? What if it was all going to go horribly wrong and she'd doomed him to some awful fate? How would she live with herself?

'Hold out your hand then,' Aunt Gretel said, as she strode to the back of the room and removed the spindle from the machine.

'Aren't you going to tell me what it is first?' the young king said.

'Certainly not. What would be the point in that, when you could still change your mind. No,' she returned to him, holding the sharpened wood out. 'You'll know soon enough.'

And with that, she took hold of the young king's strong hand, and jabbed the spindle into his fingertip, so hard that blood immediately bloomed wide, dripping onto the wooden floor below.

To give the young king his due, he didn't yelp even though it must have stung. 'Is it done?' he asked, before sucking the cut.

'It's done.' Aunt Gretel looked up at him and smiled. 'You're lucky. You chose well. A charm, not a curse. You will have a long happy marriage of contentment and all your children will be healthy.'

The young king was slightly stunned, and Rapunzel wanted to burst into joyful laughter at how clever she was. Not only was she going to marry the king, she'd also made sure their union would be a joyful one. Even though she was sure they wouldn't need the magic, it was wonderful to know for certain that they would live happily ever after.

As Aunt Gretel's words sank in, the young king began to smile too, his handsome grin showing off his perfect teeth, and this time when he looked at Rapunzel his eyes were sparkling and her heart wanted to burst into rainbow showers of colour.

'So, I may have the company of your ward for the next two evenings?' he asked. 'As per the deal?'

Aunt Gretel's mouth pursed tight before she reluctantly said, 'A deal is a deal. But she must be back by dawn.'

Twenty

Something was not right, Gretel realised as she poured a glass of wine and stared out of the kitchen window at the dark night sky. She could feel it in the pricking of her fingers and thumbs, and while on the surface there was no reason to doubt that the young king had chosen his spindle innocently enough, still she felt she'd somehow witnessed an illusion. Why was that? She ran through the events of the afternoon again, from her surprise that the young man had returned, to when she'd stabbed his finger with the spindle.

He'd been nervous, she knew that because there had been a line of tiny sweat drops around his hairline, and while the day had been warm, it hadn't been hot enough for that. She'd smelled his fear too, an emotion he wasn't used to. But had he been nervous *enough* for a man who was about to risk his very luxurious life simply for time with Rapunzel?

She'd even been afraid *for* him herself, given that she'd never expected any man to be so stupid as to agree to the deal. Why would anyone do that? No woman was so beautiful that a man would lose his senses over her unless she'd been enchanted or was one of the Sirens of the Eastern Seas or a water witch, which all amounted to the same thing.

Rapunzel was a beautiful girl, but she hadn't been enchanted, save for the creation of this curse, which Gretel was now quietly regretting having cast. It was supposed to simply entertain her for a few days and remind Rapunzel that men couldn't be trusted but now the curse was lifted and Rapunzel was out in the forest with a spoiled, young royal. Hopefully she'd stay aloof, even with all her questions about love. And why *had* she been asking all these questions so suddenly?

Taking her wine she went to Rapunzel's room and sat down heavily on the bed, and as she did, the corner of a small book poked out from under the pillow that didn't look like anything she'd have in the library. She pulled it out and stared at the luridly colourful romantic cover. What was this? How on earth could Rapunzel have it? She flicked through the pages, scanning the words full of passion and sex and ridiculous love. She had a vague memory of having thoughts like this back in a different life when she was young and stupid, before it had been proven to her that men were cruel beasts. They might disguise it around beauty for a while, but they were all monsters under the skin. Her tower was proof of that. But her Rapunzel had read this book and was now full of dangerous youthful dreams of the magic of love.

Had Conrad given it to her? For some reason that thought didn't make her as angry as she expected – Conrad existed outside of her contempt for men. He served a purpose and never crossed the line – until now. He'd been wittering about love and mistakes while that idiot spoiled king had been mooning up at the window. Gretel knew Conrad couldn't read beyond recognising the shapes of a few words, so he wouldn't have known quite how salacious the book was. Had he given it to Rapunzel as some sort of counter-balance to Gretel's own teachings? And then the young king had come along at the right time and become the focus for Rapunzel's new thinking?

It all made a terrible sense and she had a moment of blinding rage at Conrad and his ever-good intentions – for when did good ever come from good intentions – before the final piece of the puzzle slotted into place. Suddenly, Gretel knew what was making her thumbs tingle and it was nothing to do with the young man's behaviour in the spinning wheel room. It was Rapunzel's.

She got to her feet, eyes wide, reliving the coldness with which Rapunzel had made her suitor choose. Despite the coolness Gretel had taught her to show to the opposite sex, Gretel knew her ward was a kind and warm-hearted girl. Whoever the man was, whether someone she didn't like, or didn't know, or even was desperately in love with – in fact, especially if that was so – she'd have made him turn and leave. She'd have begged him *not* to let Gretel prick him with a spindle.

Rapunzel understood magic better than any whose blood was free of it, she would have known there were no curses to be taken lightly in that room. She wouldn't want anyone risking one of them for her. And yet she had. So there was only one explanation. Somehow Rapunzel had known which spindle the boy would choose and what effect it would have. She'd planned it all.

'You silly, silly girl,' Gretel hissed, as she rushed to her library, studying her books. There was disturbed dust on the very top shelf and while obvious effort had been made to create the illusion that the books hadn't been moved, they had been put back almost too neatly. Rapunzel had finally been doing her homework, but for all the wrong reasons.

Her anger cooled, shrinking to a fearful ice-block in the pit of her stomach. Irritated and let down by her ward as she was, she still didn't want Rapunzel to be hurt or in danger. She had wanted her as a companion, as a weapon for her revenge on men, but she had grown to love the girl and her desire to keep her safe from the world had left her innocently naïve. What was she doing out there? What were they *both* doing out there? She had a terrible suspicion but she needed to know for sure. She needed to *see*.

She took several deep breaths before settling into her reading chair, closing her eyes and concentrating. Her fingers twitched and her skin tingled as she called out silently into the night, hoping there would be one to answer her. The door to the library was open, and it was only a few moments before she heard the flap of wings and the rustle of feathers.

She opened her eyes and smiled at the gold and white barn owl perched beside her.

'May I?' she asked, gently, and the owl let out a soft hoot in reply.

'Thank you,' Gretel said, and she leaned back against the cushions. After a moment, her wide eyes emptied. The owl fluttered its feathers again, hopping from foot to foot, as if settling into itself, and then it spread its wings and took off, through to the hallway and then out the kitchen window and into the mystery of the night.

Twenty-One

Rapunzel could not have been happier. The air was warm, and the clearing in the forest was lit with candles everywhere and they'd eaten delicious food and drunk wine and she'd been so nervous she'd barely stopped talking while he stared at her, fascinated, and with more than a little lust. She could not imagine a better night, and, as an owl hooted overhead, she leaned forward and kissed him again, this time letting him run his hand down her body. The touch of his fingers on her neck, along with the giddying effect of the rich red wine, made her want to explode.

'You really love me?' she whispered into his ear, letting her tongue and hot breath tease him just like she'd read in the book. 'Truly.'

'Yes, yes,' he groaned, pulling her in closer. 'I'm

mad for you. I think about you constantly. I have to conquer you. I must.' His trembling hands tugged at the laces of her bodice, and she didn't stop him. This was better than the book. This was real. Someone else's hands and mouth on her skin made her feel like she was on fire.

'And we'll be so happy. When we're married,' she breathed. 'With healthy children. The charm has promised it.'

'Yes,' he breathed. 'Yes. Of course.' His words were full of distraction as he pushed up her skirt, his hands and mouth trying to be everywhere at once, and as she reached down to undo his breeches he let out a moan full of passion and then, as their bodies moved as one, all words were lost as they surrendered themselves to lust and it was so much better than she could ever have imagined, as if every star in the sky was exploding above them.

In the aftermath, they lay on the forest floor as the candles burned down, and then they did it again, and again. The air and grass were bliss on her naked skin and having learned so much about the plants and roots and herbs of the forest over the past few days, Rapunzel almost felt at one with it, as if she perhaps belonged there.

'Are there forests near your castle?' she asked,

when they were finally spent, and her head rested on the young man's strong chest.

'The Living Forest spreads into our kingdom beyond the Troll Road,' he answered, almost murmuring, almost on the edge of sleep after the wine and their exertions. 'It is a place of wonder. Rich greens and soft moss. There are several villages of huntsmen living there, people who have rarely even been into the cities.'

'Maybe we could have a cottage in the forest,' she said. 'To get away from the business of ruling sometimes. I think I would like a cottage hidden in the heart of the woods.'

'A king's place is in his castle,' her lover replied, and if she'd been less distracted by her passion and her dreams and the feel of his skin next to hers, she might have felt him stiffen slightly under her and noticed the edge of awkwardness in his voice. 'I should not have been away so long on this trip, but once I am home, my duty is there.'

'Maybe in a few years then,' she smiled up at him. 'When we have children. Before then we will have balls, and parties and guests will come in fine carriages and it will all be wonderful. I shall wear the most beautiful gowns and all your advisors will be so happy with your choice of wife.'

139

'Let's not dwell on these things.' His eyes glazed over as he ran his fingers across her alabaster skin, their bodies almost glowing in the moonlight, enjoying making her shiver. 'Tonight is for love.'

She kissed him again, their tongues teasing gently at first, then becoming more passionate, and once again they were lost in their passion.

He was so very good at it, she thought, his fingers and tongue and hands finding all the places that made her gasp, and showing her how to do the same for him while whispering sweet nothings into her ear. A naturally great lover, and even if he wasn't as witty as she'd first thought, and maybe not quite as clever, she would surely never get bored of his skilled touch? She was so very lucky and so very happy.

Nothing could go wrong.

***

Aladdin didn't need an owl's eyes to know what the young king and Rapunzel would be up to out in the forest. He knew from the stories in all the drinking taverns in Sinbad that the young king had a very healthy appetite for women, and Aladdin had played his own part in encouraging him that what he felt for Rapunzel was more than it really was. No nobleman – and

certainly no king – wanted to be thought of as lecher-
ous, even if their nature was to see every attractive
woman as a potential sexual conquest, and so Aladdin
had woven the young man's need to have Rapunzel
into a noble fantasy of love in the king's head.

It would last until his ardour cooled, which would
be at least another night. Then, when the fair maiden
from the tower was simply another notch on his
bedpost, he would make excuses about duty and his
homeland and leave her broken-hearted and definitely no longer a maiden, and give her no more thought
until he was an old man recounting his adventures to
his grandchildren. That was the path for kings and
commoners, and Rapunzel was learning it the hard
way. Aladdin was quite glad about that. He liked her.

He munched on a bun as he watched the witch's
face twitching with rage – her eyes still empty, her es-
sence far away on a branch in the forest, spying on her
ward – and took stock of how the situation was playing
out and how best he could work it to his advantage.
He could take the spindles now and make a run for
it, but the young king still had one more night with
Rapunzel and given how beautiful she was, Aladdin
doubted he'd grow bored before then. Tonight was
for teaching her, and tomorrow would be for finding
out exactly how far she'd go for him. If Aladdin fled,

the young king would want him found to appease the witch, and he didn't need any more powerful men angry with him when he could avoid it.

How best to stop the witch coming after him though, he wondered, looking thoughtfully at her bookshelves and cupboards. A witch was not an enemy he wanted.

And then it came to him. A way to thank Rapunzel for everything she'd done for him and an escape plan all rolled into one.

All he needed to do was create some chaos. By the time the dust settled, he'd be long gone, and once he had the genie in his control, nothing else would matter anyway.

When he slid once more under the bed, Gretel waking with a scream of rage, he couldn't help but smile at his own ingenuity despite his loathing of the cramped surroundings. This was all going to be quite, quite brilliant.

***

When the air began to cool in the hour just before dawn, they dressed reluctantly and began their slow wander back to the white tower, arms wrapped around each other and limbs aching pleasantly. Only then did Rapunzel feel the first knot of worry about what she was going to say to Aunt Gretel.

She had to be honest about her feelings. She would explain that the young king had been wonderful, and that she'd kissed him – nothing more – and that she thought she loved him. Aunt Gretel would be angry, she knew that, but maybe after a second night with the king with no mishaps, Aunt Gretel would realise that there was space in the world for true love after all. She'd understand that Rapunzel couldn't stay locked up in the tower for the rest of her life simply because the world had done something to Gretel so many years ago to make her hate men. Her Aunt Gretel loved her, she knew that. And surely she'd want her to be happy. She could come and live with them in the castle and they'd all be happy together.

'Until tonight, then,' the young king said and kissed her lips, which were almost bruised from so much kissing.

'I can't wait,' Rapunzel answered. And it was true. One more night and then a lifetime as his wife and the queen of a whole kingdom. She loved him so much that watching him walk away felt like something tearing inside her.

She hoped he'd turn back and wave and grin, but he didn't, and that hurt too. But perhaps, she told herself, as the door to the tower opened, that would be too painful for him. He was a strong king. However much he loved her – which she was sure he must do, after everything they'd done together in the night – he couldn't show weakness.

Twenty-Two

Her aunt was so angry that all the candles sconced in the walls of the tower went out for a moment, leaving the inner rooms in complete darkness, and then burst into such bright flames that Rapunzel had to squint through her tears as Aunt Gretel raged, her face as purple as a fresh beet.

'Everything I taught you, gone! Just like that!' She snapped her fingers. 'All these years and I've raised a fool who lets her head be turned by the first handsome man to lie to her. You gave it all away without a second thought. To a shallow, vain, spoiled *boy*-king.'

'I only kissed him,' Rapunzel said through her sobs.

'Yes, you only kissed him and he chose that spindle entirely by chance. I *know* you're lying to me, Rapunzel.' There was hurt in Aunt Gretel's anger, and that only made Rapunzel feel worse. Why couldn't she understand? Rapunzel didn't want to hurt her, she just wanted to be happy.

'I love him. And he loves me. Why can't you be pleased for me? We're going to be married.'

Gretel stared at her, wide-eyed for a long moment and then barked an unpleasant laugh. 'That's what he's told you, is it?'

'In as many words, yes.'

'He doesn't love you, Rapunzel,' Gretel snorted. 'How can he? How can you love him? You don't even know each other.'

'True love doesn't work like that!' She knew she sounded petulant but her aunt was making her feel like a child, not a grown woman.

'True love is a rare beast, Rapunzel.' The rage in Aunt Gretel's voice faded, replaced by something close to disappointment. 'It's a magic. True love is the only thing that can break a curse. This is not true love – this is youthful stupidity. This is a man lying for his own gain. Yes, he thinks you're beautiful. But he does not love you. All he sees of you is beauty. And he's had that now. Back in his own kingdom he has a full life.' She paused. 'He probably already has a wife.'

'What would you know about love?' Rapunzel's face burned as her own anger flared up. 'You've hidden in a tower all your life hating people and trying to make me just like you! Why should I be that way? Why would I *want* to be that way? I don't want to be like you! I *pity* you!'

The colour drained from Aunt Gretel's face but Rapunzel was too caught up in her own hurt to care about the barbs she'd thrown. She ran to her room and slammed the door, throwing herself down onto her bed and sobbing harder than she had since she'd first been abandoned by her father in his crimson jacket.

Aunt Gretel didn't follow her, and, after a few minutes, Aladdin crawled out from under the bed and gave her some of his water. She sipped it and wiped her nose with the back of her hand.

'You won't be able to do that when you're Queen of the High Born,' he said, with a chuckle, and she forced herself to smile a little despite the ache in her throat from crying.

'Maybe she's right,' Rapunzel snuffled. 'Maybe the king doesn't love me. What do I know of men and love anyway? Only what I read in that silly book.'

'Oh, he loves you.' Aladdin took her hand and squeezed it, his young face earnest. 'It's in the way he looks at you. He can't sleep or eat without you. He can't exist without you.' His voice was gentle and soothing as he rested her head on his lap, stroking the top of her head, calming the strands of hair coming loose from her plait. 'In all my adventures this is the first time I've seen true love. Soon, he'll lead you to his castle on a white pony and you will bind yourselves to marriage with the dragon oath and you will be the most beloved queen his kingdom has ever known.'

'Do you really think so?' She sniffed again, her tears drying. Aladdin had a knack for making her feel better. He'd told her he was fifteen, still older than she'd thought, but much younger than her, but he'd adventured throughout the world. She trusted him.

'I do.' He paused, hesitating, as if a sudden thought was striking him, before he added, 'And maybe there's a way to prove to your Aunt Gretel that he loves you too. To prove without doubt that he sees past your beauty.'

'What do you mean?' Rapunzel sat up, staring into his brown eyes.

'No, it's too much.' He shook his head. 'It's probably stupid.'

'Tell me.' She squeezed his hand. 'If you have a way to help me, I must know of it.'

'All right,' Aladdin said, and after a deep breath, he explained his thinking to her, talking in a low whisper as if worried Aunt Gretel could hear him from her library.

When he'd finished, Rapunzel's head reeled with the audacity of it. 'Aunt Gretel would never agree,' she said, almost breathless.

'She'd have to.' Aladdin's eyes sparkled with excitement. 'Don't you see? She wouldn't have a choice. To say no would be akin to admitting that you're right and that the king *does* love you for you and not just your beauty, and that she's keeping you here because she's lonely and wants you to be the same. She has to see it for herself. With her own eyes.'

'Not exactly her own eyes,' Rapunzel said and they both smiled, and Rapunzel's heart beat faster as the plan solidified in her head. It would work. It absolutely would.

'Thank you, Aladdin.' She planted a kiss on his cheek and pulled him in close for a tight hug. 'I think I had a best friend before, in my old life. Sometimes I get glimpses of her. Dark hair with blonde stripes in it. I loved her very much. Even though I don't really remember her, somehow I feel you're similar.' She sat back, her tears gone. 'You're my new best friend and I'm very lucky to have met you.'

'You're my best friend too.' Aladdin answered and hugged her back. 'And I want you to be happy.'

***

'You can't be serious,' Aunt Gretel said, and if her face had been purple when Rapunzel had got back to the tower, it was ash-pale now. 'That's a ridiculous suggestion.'

'No, it's not. It's the best way to find out if you're right or I am. See if he can tell the difference. If he really loves me, as I believe he does, he'll realise you're not me when you're together. Or at least realise that something is wrong. And if I'm right then you have to promise to give me your blessing and be happy for me.' She looked earnestly at her aunt. 'Because I want you to be happy too. And you could come and live with us and—'

'And if I'm right?' Aunt Gretel cut her off, mid-sentence. 'What then?'

Rapunzel stood taller, defiant. 'You won't be.'

'But if I am?'

'Then I'll apologise and never deceive you again and send him packing.'

Aunt Gretel nodded, almost persuaded. 'Let me think on it. I'll give you my answer this afternoon. Go and rest, child. You need sleep in order to keep your wits about you.'

Rapunzel nodded and went back to her room, Aladdin safely hidden under the bed again, happy that Aunt Gretel was at least in part mollified, but concerned at how pale she had turned. She'd almost looked afraid, and Rapunzel had never seen Aunt Gretel afraid of anything. As far as Gretel was concerned, people should be afraid of *her*, not the other way around. But then, Rapunzel thought as she lay her suddenly very tired head on the pillow, it was easy to be unafraid when you never left your home.

How many years had Gretel been here? Witches lived longer and aged slower, that's what she always said. How long had it been since she'd walked further than the flower and herb gardens surrounding the tower? Ten years? Twenty? More? Let alone walked and talked with a handsome man? *Any* man? The only villager she ever saw was Conrad and that was because they needed him and he somehow refused to be put off by Gretel's abrasiveness and Rapunzel's own aloof deportment.

It'd be good for Aunt Gretel, she decided as she drifted into sleep.

To see the good in people.

To see that true love is real.

Twenty-Three

Gretel couldn't do it. She couldn't. Leave the tower? Her breath choked in her lungs just thinking about it. She was afraid. Yes, she was afraid. To go out at night with a man? Into the forest? A young handsome man full of flattering words? Oh, such danger. Her racing pulse was a warning knell as she fought to catch her breath, panic threatening to unthread her.

The memories came flooding back, bubbling up from the deep place inside her, the place of once upon a time, long ago that she tried to forget had ever been more than a dream. A time when she was not the witch of the white tower, but simply Gretel. Oh, so long ago, and yet also now, as she was lost in it again, like yesterday.

MAGIC

Her childhood.
The story that had brought her here.

***

When those from other kingdoms thought of the Winter Lands they would speak of ice and hard rocks and snow and burnings, but those born and raised there knew that while the winters were indeed long and hard, the months from April to June, when the ground thawed and the crops burst into life and the river glittered and the trout swam, were the most beautiful in all the Nine Kingdoms.

Her mother had told Gretel, when she was very small, that the rarer a thing was the more beautiful and valuable it became. That was how it was with summer in the Winter Lands and that was how it was with her. Gretel believed it about her homelands, but didn't believe it about herself.

As she grew, she knew she was not pretty like the other girls who were blooming into womanhood. She was shorter than them, and solid, and had what would be kindly called a homely, ruddy face, and if it weren't for her ice-blue eyes that were almost violet in their flecks, and her ice-blonde hair, there would be nothing distinguishing about her at all.

Her father was a tailor and spinning wheel maker, a small and rat-like man who was not kind to Gretel or her mother.

When the other girls went to dances in the town square, Gretel would spend her evenings stitching or weaving or repurposing old wool for him, and her mind would wander to all the handsome young men of the town and wish that one would look her way – especially Jon, the painter's son – even though she knew her father had his eye on Rudy, the butcher's boy, for her. He was a steady dullard, but their union would put meat on the table through the long winter months. If truth be told, she was sure the disappointment would flow both ways, but she also knew that Jon and his friends would never look her way other than to laugh like the girls did. The plain tailor's daughter who dressed in clothes that didn't quite fit or suit her, but that her father insisted she wore as a reluctant mannequin for his work, as if he made sure that the dresses – while fine - were always slightly too small so she wouldn't cost him so much in food, and she was always hungry in the hope that the fabric would stop pinching her stocky body. Her father's lack of love for her was clear for all the town to see.

She would rather have been invisible than the subject of mockery, but it was her lot and, despite her daydreams, by the time she was fourteen, she was trying to make her peace with it. Perhaps the butcher's boy would be kind even if he wasn't clever or handsome. She could live with kindness. It was more than her mother had been blessed with in marriage.

MAGIC

As with many stories, everything changed with a single drop of blood.

Sometimes, even so many years later, Gretel could still feel the sharpness of the spindle that she'd carved too sharp and the brightness of the red – so bright it looked like it glittered – as it spilled heavily onto the material folded carefully beside her station. Her father turned, enraged that she could have stained cloth that had been paid for, and he had hit her twice before her mother gave a whisper of dread and said, 'Look.'

Gretel's father's rage evaporated as he saw the blood on the fabric disappear to nothing before the material shimmered slightly brighter than it should.

'That can't be,' he said, quietly, but already his mind was whirring with possibilities, with the truth of what he was seeing. 'The girl's a witch,' he said eventually, stunned, voicing aloud the word that Gretel and her timid mother didn't dare speak, and Gretel immediately burst into tears with the horror of it.

'We must hide it,' her mother said, more assertive than Gretel had ever heard her. 'No one must know. We will never speak of this again.'

'They'll burn me,' Gretel cried. 'They'll cut off my fingers and burn me alive.'

Her mother pulled her close and held her. 'No, they will not. We'll destroy this cloth and weave some more and we will take extra care that your blood doesn't spill. Perhaps we could move? Go to the Eastern Seas or into the forest where you will be safe and can live freely.' She was talking fast, fear clear in her voice, but her words comforted Gretel. Her mother loved her. She would keep her safe.

'Don't be a fool,' her father snapped. *'There's gold to be made here.'*

They looked at him in horror. *'But magic is forbidden in the Winter Lands. They'll put her to death if they find out. And us too, perhaps.'*

Their fear was rightly placed, for everyone in the kingdom knew that the king, whose grandfather had been told that one day their line would be deposed and the Winter Lands ruled by witches' blood, was even more ruthless about magic than his father before him.

A dragon had screeched over the castle in the year of Gretel's birth, a mighty storm following in the wake of its wings, a true sign of a new pure witch being born, and so the soldiers had always been seeking her, alert for enchantments.

'They won't find out.' He was already pacing, his fingers twitching in the way they always did when he was thinking about money. *'Not if we're careful. We live far from the castle. We're a forgotten town. Imagine how much people would pay for a cursed spinning wheel? A charmed blanket?'*

MAGIC

'They'll pay in any of the other kingdoms too,' Gretel's mother pleaded.

Her father shook his head. 'Not as much as here. Not when it's forbidden.'

Gretel listened in terror as her mother tried to reason with her father, begging him to think of their safety, but then her father dragged his wife into the bedroom and beat her so soundly that it was two days before she could even sip broth through her bruises. She never fully recovered, fading away and dying within months, even when Gretel tried to charm her into surviving.

Her magic was so new to her and her terror of being caught made it weaker, and her mother wished so hard to be free of life that even years later, when Gretel had mastered her power, she thought no charm would ever have worked. Perhaps her mother had hidden magic of her own and in those final weeks she turned it inwards against herself.

After that, when she remembered those final two years of her father and her, it was as if everything was wrapped in a dark cloud. Her father made spinning wheels and spindles, and Gretel would curse or charm them to order and then her father would sit up at night counting the rapidly gathering gold he kept hidden under the floorboards.

By the time she was seventeen, Gretel was almost as cowed as her mother had been, and the knot of terror in her stomach, fear of both her father and the burning, grew so

157

much she didn't even crave the sweet cakes that her mother had occasionally let her have. Each day vanished into the grey routine of cooking and cleaning and learning about magic from the forbidden books her father bought her – the only time he spent money on anything for her – so that she could work more precise charms, before weaving and sewing and spilling her blood for her father's profit.

Then, in the depths of winter, a rose of hope bloomed.

She was at the market, carefully choosing apples for her father, making sure there wasn't the hint of a bruise that could result in bruises on her, when someone nudged her as they passed, sending her basket of purchases tumbling to the ground. She was almost in tears with panic as she crouched to gather the bread and vegetables from the muddy snow, so terrified to see that two eggs had broken that when strong hands took the basket from her she almost shrieked thinking that it was her father and he was going to beat her in front of the whole village.

'Allow me. It was my fault. I'm so sorry.' It wasn't her father's voice. This voice was like melted chocolate on a freezing day or the first pink bud of blossom appearing on a tree. She looked up, and couldn't find her voice. It was Jon, the painter's son, and he was smiling at her apologetically, holding her arm to help her to her feet. 'And I will replace those eggs. I'm so clumsy. My father is always telling me off for treading paint onto the floorboards.' He repacked her

basket and handed it back to her. 'It's Gretel, isn't it? I've seen you around.'

He did more than replace the eggs. He walked with her, nearly all the way home until she told him not to come any nearer in case her father saw them together. He was spending more and more time in the ale houses these days but those hours only made him meaner. He hadn't mentioned Rudy, the butcher's son, and his proposal for some weeks now and she was starting to think that he would never release her and there was nothing she could do about it. Her father was mean, but he was not stupid, and one of the first charms he'd made her cast was that she could never curse him. She knew it was unlikely that she'd ever see Jon alone again and that he was just being polite, so she didn't want this wonderful moment to be marred by her father's vicious temper.

But it was not the last time she saw Jon alone.

As the long winter stretched on and the blanket of snow that covered the village grew thicker and icier, she often found him waiting at the market for her, and they would walk the long way home, and sometimes pause at the baker's and he would buy them both a hot pastry and they would burn their tongues and laugh, and despite still grieving for her mother and having to live with her cruel and miserly father, Gretel found she was happy. She sang quietly to herself while she worked, and sometimes Jon would walk past her window and smile and she could almost forget the terrible secret she carried. They were all older now and the girls laughed at her less, occupied with their own court-ships. She was a forgotten thing, poor Gretel, the cruel tailor's daughter. But she did not feel like poor Gretel. She felt like the happiest girl in the world.

After a few weeks, Jon kissed her under the trees at the edge of the forest and she realised she was in love. He made her skin warm and stole her sleep and she couldn't keep from smiling, but all the time her secret grew like a worm inside her.

It was worse now too, as there were whispers that magic was afoot in their corner of the Winter Lands. Goats and sheep were sick. Others had runs of bad luck that were not normal. People muttered of curses.

One day, a late afternoon, after her father had pushed her to her limits and her fingertips hurt from pricking and her arms had bruises from shaking, her secret spilled out as Jon held her and asked her what was wrong. He listened as she told him everything, about her father's beatings, how her mother died after they found out she was a witch, how he made her do magic, how he kept his gold under the floor-board in his bedroom and loved counting it more than he ever loved her or her mother and that he'd never set her free.

Jon was shocked, she could see that, but just as she was wishing she could take the words back, he kissed her eyelids *and said he'd keep her secret, and held her so tight she almost couldn't breathe with the relief of it all. He said he had to go but to meet him the next night under the old oak in the middle of the village and they would leave.*

That was when they came – as she waited for him filled with excitement and with a pouch of gold coins she'd taken from her father's hoard, hers by right anyway – their torches flaming in the night.

She'd smelled the fire before she'd seen it, heard their tread before they appeared, but she hadn't moved until the night sky was bright with flames, and then – only when she'd seen that Jon was right there amongst them, alongside his father and Rudy, the butcher's boy, and saw that any affection he had for her was gone, an illusion, that it had all perhaps been a trick – only then, as the first hand reached for her, baying for her burning, did she turn and run.

She ran for what felt like for ever, darting down alleys and shouting curses that meant nothing but cleared towns-folk from her path, horror in their faces at the fact that a witch had been among them, until she reached the woods, and with the shouts of 'Find the witch! Burn her!' following close, she ran into the trees, shrugging off her heavy coat to move faster.

Winter branches lacerated her face and arms, but as her blood spilled into the snow, the forest chose to save her. Where trees parted for her, they tightened around her pursuers, old roots rising up to trip and tangle, and after a while, as her exhaustion over rode her blinding panic, she realised there were no blazing fires behind her and she could no longer hear the terrifying calls to kill her.

The earth beneath her grew less frozen as she trudged onwards, and eventually, after nearly two full days and nights of walking, she reached a clearing near a stream and collapsed there.

She thought she might die. She hoped she would. But when she woke, the sun was shining and wild flowers and peonies were blooming, and she decided she was far enough away from her village to be safe. This was not the Winter Lands, the green grass beneath her in March told her that. The forest had saved her and in the forest she would stay, but never again would she trust the world of men and she would never let her heart love again.

As her blood dripped into the soil, she spun her white tower from the magic, a safe haven – and there she would stay.

Quietly, it became a home, and she used her gold coins wisely, and news of the witch of the white tower spread, but Jon and the others never came with torches again.

They couldn't – she had seen to that.

She had sent a bird with a message to the King of the Winter Lands, reporting that the town had harboured a witch and made easy with magic. Spies sent into the taverns *and ale houses found that it was true and all the men of the town, smug with their stolen shares of her father's hidden gold, were burned in her stead for not telling their king. They found her father locked in a cell in the sheriff's house and they took him to the city, where he was beaten to death, screaming for his daughter, the witch, to save him.*

Her mother would have approved of that.

But sometimes – still, after everything – she would dream of Jon's kiss and her cold heart would break all over again.

***

'Aunt Gretel?'

Rapunzel's voice jolted her back to the present and, seeing her ward's young beautiful face so full of hope, Gretel knew she had no choice, despite her heart hammering with fear. 'I'll do it. But I do it because I love you.'

They waited until dusk, and then Rapunzel brought the spindle down to the study and the two women sat face to face.

'For the glimmer to work we must both prick our fingers and wish for it. The spell will last until dawn, then we will return to ourselves.'

'Will we feel any different?' Rapunzel asked, and her Aunt Gretel shrugged.

163

'I've never glimmered. But I doubt it. It's an illusory spell only. A surface thing.' She looked tired. 'Are you sure you want to do this?'

'Yes,' Rapunzel answered, firmly, and then she pricked her finger and wished hard, before passing the spindle to Aunt Gretel to do the same. Just as the sun set, they both closed their eyes.

Rapunzel felt the change before she saw it. Her bones were suddenly lead-heavy, as was her skin, and there was something else, a deep ache in the heart of her that was different. She opened her eyes and gasped, seeing her own face looking back at her, equally shocked. 'I feel different,' Rapunzel said with her aunt's voice. 'So very strange.'

'So do I.' Her aunt looked down at her slim young hands. 'But we will be back to ourselves soon enough.' She stood up and smoothed down the pretty dress Rapunzel had chosen for her to wear and for a moment Rapunzel wished she'd never touched the spindle, even though that was silly. She and her aunt had swapped appearances and that was bound to be unsettling, but it was for true love, and when she was proved right these strange aches and pains would be worth it.

At the sound of horse's hooves from outside, she got up, wobbling slightly with the new weight she had to carry, and the two of them went to her bedroom – Rapunzel, in her aunt's body, leading the way in case Aladdin had snuck out – and stood at the window. The young king approached from below and her heart leapt. It took all her effort not to smile at him. Instead, she maintained Aunt Gretel's stern expression, and looked upon him with disdain.

'You may have your second night,' she called down. 'And then, if you are both truly in love, I will not stand in the way of the marriage.' She wished she could see his face more clearly but he was hidden in shadow.

She stayed at the window until she'd watched her love walking into the forest with Aunt Gretel disguised in her skin and her heart ached with envy. Behind her, the boy shuffled out from under her bed.

'No more confined spaces as long as I breathe,' he muttered, his back cracking as he straightened. 'A castle, that's where I shall live.'

'You can come and stay with me when I'm queen,' she said. 'In fact, I shall command it.' She smiled at him and he laughed in return.

'Look at you. Transformed. All your youth swallowed up.'

'Stop it.' She rolled her eyes at him. 'It's strange enough being *in* here without you making it worse.

I didn't think I'd *feel* like her. I'm even craving something sweet.' She sat down on the bed, forlorn. 'Do you think he's tried to kiss her already, Aladdin? How long will it take him to realise something's not right?' She lay back like a petulant child, hitting the covers with her hands. 'It's so unbearable. I hate this not knowing, and they've only been gone a few minutes.'

'Then summon an owl and look through its eyes. That's what she did last night.'

Rapunzel sat straight up again, aghast. 'She was watching me? Everything I did?'

'I didn't want to tell you when you were so upset, but an owl came and then when it flew away she didn't move for a very long time. So maybe you try the same?'

'How?' she asked.

'You're the witch right now,' he said with a grin. 'So just try it.'

Twenty-Four

Despite how she seemed from Rapunzel's young perspective, Gretel wasn't an old woman, but as she walked through the woods with the young king, she was surprised at how young she felt in Rapunzel's skin. Without the weight in her bones it was like she was walking on air, her limbs felt so light. She'd always presumed the weightiness had been the same for everyone, but now, as she breathed in the warm air, she realised that having bones so heavy must come from the magic. The joy at her freedom of movement almost countered her fear of being so far from the safety of her white tower.

She glanced over her shoulder, and was glad that she could still see the top of it through the canopy of leaves, a light glowing from Rapunzel's window like a lighthouse off the Meridien Isles.

'You're very quiet tonight.' She smiled up at the handsome man beside her and softened towards her young ward. Of course Rapunzel was dazzled by him. What young woman wouldn't be? Strangely, all her own animosities towards men had also faded somewhat with the glimmer. Perhaps inhabiting Rapunzel's body meant she'd also left some of her trauma behind, and when the young king reached for her hand she let him take it – as she knew she had to for their deception to work – and she found she enjoyed it, even if it gave her a pang of sadness for her one glimpse of love so many years ago. Jon was the last man to hold her hand like this, before he betrayed her.

'I'm sad because my adventures are coming to an end and I must give up forest floors for the formality of castle life and kingship.'

Gretel almost imitated Rapunzel in a gush over the wondrousness of palace life but remembered her task. How long would it take him to feel there was something different – *off* – about his one true love? To realise he'd been tricked by a witch?

There was a feast laid out as there had been the night before, with jugged wine and an array of delicious foods, and as they sat on the blanket, for once her eyes didn't wander straight to the sweet pastries.

She didn't crave them at all. This glimmer was strange indeed and not at all what she expected. It didn't feel like an illusion but rather that she was fully inhabiting Rapunzel's body. The young king filled a goblet of wine and passed it to her.

'Yes, it must be very restrictive,' she said after a large swallow. 'All those ministers telling you what to do all the time. Boring dinners with visiting dignitaries. So tiresome. Perhaps when I'm living there too, it will be different.'

'Yes.' He leaned forward, looking into her eyes, and, despite herself, she shivered.

All this time she'd thought she didn't need the outside world, but the night air on her skin was wonderful. To be surrounded by the wildness of nature was wonderful. And, she thought, taking another sip, this wine was pretty good too. Somewhere overhead a bird's feathers rustled in the branches.

'But let's not think about that now.' The young king traced his fingers gently across her bottom lip, and a chain-reaction of electric sparks exploded through her body, leaving her breathless, and then his mouth was on hers and all thought vanished. For a moment, time unwound, and it was Jon kissing her again, and she was young and full of hope. In everything that came afterwards, she had forgotten how wonderful those moments had made her feel. How alive.

'No,' she said, breaking away momentarily, despite her young body reacting instinctively to his touch. 'Let's not. Talk of castles bores me. I can't be doing with all that ridiculous finery.' Gretel paused, looking for a reaction from him because from what she'd observed the previous night, talk of castles very much did *not* bore Rapunzel, but there was nothing. All he wanted to do was kiss her again, and she let him, her skin unbearably hot in a way she hadn't felt in a lifetime. Was it wrong to do this, she wondered as her hands reached up and pulled him towards her. Probably. Not least because she wasn't who he thought she was. But that was the point, wasn't it? Surely, if he loved Rapunzel he would see a difference between them in the way they kissed or touched as well as talked? And she found, as she felt the weight of his body leaning onto hers, she wanted his touch – *Jon's* touch, from when she thought he loved her – very much indeed.

***

Aladdin had to admit, Rapunzel had taken to magic like a duck to water. The owl had come as swiftly as it had for Gretel the night before, and after a couple of failed attempts, the girl had realised she had to ask the owl's permission to see through its eyes, and then both she and the owl were gone.

He clicked his fingers in front of her eyes a couple of times but they didn't even flicker, and then he relaxed. He had time. Rapunzel would want to watch everything and she wouldn't be back before Gretel was, and by then he'd be long gone through the forest. He wished he could stay and watch his game play out, but his adventure was elsewhere, with the Great Magician and the genie. He kissed Rapunzel on the cheek – he really had enjoyed her company – and then set about his business.

He found a hessian bag in the kitchen and went to the spindle room and took five of the enchanted spindles, scratching them with markings so he knew which was which, should he need to, as well as a few of the ordinary ones waiting for enchantment. He left the spinning wheels behind. He'd thought of taking one, but the weight would slow him down, and he only needed to look as if he'd brought a sackful of magical items for a few moments – after that, neither he nor the Great Magician would have need of them for very different reasons.

He grabbed several of Gretel's cakes and a small bottle of wine and then carefully left a note on Rapunzel's bed before he crept down the stairs, whispered 'Open Sesame' and disappeared into the night, the young king's knife in his belt.

Maybe she'd understand and maybe she wouldn't. He'd never liked a person before and wasn't really sure how giving a gift should work. At least he hadn't killed her. That was something.

He was in such a good mood that for a moment he considered not killing the young king's mercenaries. Then, he decided, surely he deserved a treat?

***

As she pulled her clothes back around her, Gretel was at once happy that she'd finally experienced physical love and sad that she'd hidden away from life for so long. She was in no way enamoured of the young king, but she had very much enjoyed touching and being touched, and she'd had all the confidence of pretending to be someone else while doing it, both her and not her. What a strange life it was. Her heart also ached very much for Rapunzel.

She had said several very unromantic things – she didn't want children, wasn't really sure about *obeying* a husband whether king or not, and when she'd picked up a cake and said 'Oh, my favourite,' he hadn't commented that, unlike Gretel, Rapunzel had no sweet tooth and never ate cakes. In fact, he seemed to know very little about Rapunzel at all. She also noted that he didn't ask any questions of her either. Not a single one. Even Jon, before his fear of her witchcraft overtook his feelings for her, had been full of questions, wanting to know her. This young man certainly wanted Rapunzel, but he didn't love her, Gretel was more and more sure of it.

Now that their love-making was over, he once again avoided her gaze as she talked about the future.

'Do you think your advisors will like me?' she asked, and he shrugged, uncomfortable, as she let out a loud belch in a very un-Rapunzel way.

'It might be better if I go ahead and prepare them,' he said. 'You know, just in case they react badly. They will expect me to marry a noble woman or princess and so this will be a shock.' He poured himself more wine and looked down into the goblet. 'I'll come back for you, of course.' The words were paper thin, and while they might convince a girl desperate to believe him, they certainly didn't work on Gretel.

'Maybe we shouldn't get married at all,' she said, matter-of-fact, picking at a piece of cheese.

He looked up at her, surprised, and with more than a smidgen of hope. 'What do you mean?'

'It seems silly now.' She shrugged. 'I mean, all this has been great, but do we really want each other for the rest of our lives? I don't really know you and you don't really know me.'

'Oh, I'm so glad you said that.' He held her hands tightly with the first real affection of the evening. 'I thought it was only me feeling that way and I wasn't sure how to say it.' He shrugged as his words trailed away and Gretel almost snorted with laughter. The relief coming from him was palpable.

'It's all right,' she squeezed his hand. 'True love is very rare after all. And I expect your advisors already have a bride picked out for you.'

'Yes, they do.' He at least looked slightly shame-faced. 'The wedding is all planned for my return.'

Gretel felt another surge of pity for Rapunzel. He was never going to marry her, even if he'd momentarily convinced himself he might. All he'd really wanted was one last adventure.

'At least I freed you from the witch,' he said.

'Yes,' she smiled. 'There is that.' She ate another chunk of cheese as they sat in the easy silence of people whose passions have been spent and who have been honest with each other. 'When will you leave?'

'Dawn.'

They looked at each other for a long moment, and even though she knew for sure that he didn't love Rapunzel, she found herself hoping that he'd at least comment that she'd been different tonight, but still he did not. Instead, he talked of himself and his journey home and she could hear his longing for the life waiting for him in his voice. He had done well, she mused. Given the charm in the spindle Rapunzel had chosen for him, he knew the bride waiting for him at his castle would give him a happy marriage and healthy children. Oh, Rapunzel, she thought. What a mistake to make.

They said their farewells, shared an awkward kiss, and she noted that the lust had gone from his touch, these two nights having already provided him with everything he wanted from her. She mulled on Conrad's words when they'd walked in the gardens. How youth had to make mistakes. People needed them in order to know when something was real and good for them rather than a fantasy. She would break it gently to the girl, she decided as she walked back towards the tower. And life would change for them both from now on. It was time to let the past go and embrace the future. The young king was not wicked or cruel. He was spoiled, yes, and foolish, but Rapunzel would get over him and perhaps one day, when she was happy in a marriage of her own, they might laugh about it together, this folly of youth.

It was time to set Rapunzel free to find her own destiny.

Twenty-Five

Rapunzel, in the kitchen with cake crumbs around her mouth, burst into tears as soon as Gretel had run up the tower stairs, two at a time, still enjoying the lightness of her limbs, and found her. It was strange seeing herself crying like a child, and her heart went out to the younger woman inside her older body. She found herself softening the truth to protect her hurt feelings.

'He's been called back to the castle,' she said, trying to comfort her ward. 'He didn't want to go but—'

'*I saw everything*,' Rapunzel cut in, her voice tart as a sour apple. 'With an owl. Just like you did. I know what he said. What he did. How relieved he was when you said he didn't have to marry me.' She stormed into her room and sat down, heavily, on the bed.

'Oh.' Gretel sat beside her. 'I'm sorry.'

'No, you're not. You must be laughing at me for being such a fool.'

If Gretel was feeling some of Rapunzel's natural joyfulness then it seemed that while she was in Gretel's body, Rapunzel had a share of Gretel's bitterness at the world.

'I am absolutely not and I'm annoyed at myself for so wanting to prove a point to you that I didn't wonder if maybe I was wrong. '

'You weren't wrong. He didn't love me.' Rapunzel shrugged Gretel's arm away.

'But neither do you love him, not really. It was an infatuation for both of you. An illusion of love. A glimmer of its own.'

Gretel gently turned Rapunzel to face her. Outside, the first birds started their morning song. Soon the glimmer would be over and she would be herself again, heavy, aching bones and all, but she was determined to hold on to this positivity of spirit. Maybe she'd even tell Rapunzel the truth about her father. That maybe he hadn't returned because he couldn't, rather than didn't want to. The trust he had placed in her. The trust she had broken. The haunting rattle of his name.

'And that is fine. The hurt will ease. You will meet more handsome men and one of them will be your true love. But if you don't make these mistakes then you won't know the right one when he finally comes along . . . This is all my fault.' She brushed a strand of ice-white hair from Rapunzel's eyes. 'You would have known more of the world if I hadn't been so keen for you to hide away from it as I have. I've been afraid of letting anyone hurt me ever again, which has not only wasted years of my own life, but kept you from living yours too. Things are going to change, Rapunzel. I promise you. As soon as dawn comes and we are ourselves again, we will sleep and then perhaps go into the village. Together.'

Rapunzel finally laid her head on Gretel's shoulder and let out a weepy sigh. 'I thought it was going to be so perfect.'

'So little in life ever is. But perfect would be very dull indeed.'

She looked out of the window at the first streak of blue in the sky and closed her eyes, ready for the glimmer to end.

***

The young king hadn't realised how much he'd been looking forward to getting home until he'd saddled up his horse as dawn was breaking and said goodbye to

Conrad. The older man had asked if he'd said farewell to Rapunzel and he was glad he could say that they were parting as friends. Everything had worked out well, he thought happily as he trotted into the forest, and he could go back to his kingdom with a tale of deceiving a witch. And it was his to tell, without the duke having supervised him. That would impress his young bride – he was sure of it as long as he left some parts out. He found, as daylight broke, that he had some excitement at the prospect of his impending wedding too, especially since he knew – thanks to the spindle Rapunzel had chosen for him – that it would be a happy marriage.

It was a smug happiness he was enjoying as he arrived at the spot where his mercenaries had been camped, ready to pay them to escort him all the way to the border. Only the mercenaries were gone, although the embers of the fire in the middle of the small clearing were still warm, and their horses were still tied to the branches of a tree. As he approached one, it reared up, spooked by something, and it was then that the young king saw smears of blood leading to a huntsman's pit on the far side. When he looked over the edge and saw the red mess that was left of his soldiers, any pride in his own achievements was wiped right out of his mind.

He staggered backwards, shocked and terrified, and fell into the mossy base of a tree nearby. Who could have done this terrible thing? Who had the skill to murder six hardened mercenaries with such brutality? As he trembled, getting his breath back, and the sun broke overhead, he saw the glint of gold tossed in a patch of briars by the hunting pit. When he'd calmed enough to stand, he went to look, and his horror doubled as he picked the item up. It was his own royal dagger, sticky with drying blood. He threw up then, right there on the spot, and then washed the knife in the stream, knowing he couldn't return to the castle without it, and got back on his horse and rode fast, without stopping, all the way home.

He did not stop to look for Aladdin.

He never wanted to see Aladdin again.

***

The light had changed but they hadn't, and Gretel was beginning to get a very uneasy feeling in the pit of the stomach that wasn't hers. She knew her magic and she knew every spell she had cast, and the glimmer should have broken with the first ray of sunshine. It should never have felt the way it did. The glimmer was an illusory spell. Neither of them should have *felt* any different – and yet they did.

'I don't understand it,' she muttered.

'What's happened?' Rapunzel stood up, looking down at Gretel's body and then, aghast, at Gretel. 'Why am I still you?'

Gretel didn't answer but looked at her ward as a thought struck her. 'What did you mean when you said you used an owl? Like me? How did you know I owl-watched you?'

Rapunzel didn't answer, her mouth opening and closing like a stunned goldfish, and Gretel didn't wait for her to push out an answer, but instead hurried to her library. She opened her cabinet and pulled out the vial of blood she kept at the back. It was half-empty. 'Did you use this?' She spun around, holding it up to Rapunzel. 'Tell me you didn't put it on the glimmer spindle? Or the young king's charm? Nothing good comes from too much blood, you know that!'

'No, I didn't. I wouldn't!' She paused. 'Oh no . . .' Rapunzel's hand flew to her mouth and her eyes widened. '*Aladdin*.'

She ran up the stairs as fast as Gretel's heavy legs would take her and then Gretel heard another anguished exclamation. What had the girl done?

'He's taken some of the spindles. And the glimmer

was his idea! He told me to make you do it.' The words came out in a rush and Gretel desperately tried to make sense of what she was saying as Rapunzel raced past her into her room, looking under the bed. She sat back on her heels and started to cry again. 'He's gone. He was under the bed, and now he's gone.'

Gretel came closer, a small piece of paper on Rapunzel's pillow catching her eye. She picked it up and saw, scrawled in a flamboyant hand, *'You deserve a life less ordinary.'*

She turned, as the pieces of what had happened started to slot into place, and sank to the floor beside her ward. 'Oh, Rapunzel,' she breathed out the words with a woe-filled sigh. 'What did you do?'

Twenty-Six

Aladdin was glad to be back in the warm salty air of Sinbad with sand between his toes and the smells of a million spices, street-baked foods and a fair amount of shit all competing in the air with the noise and business of a city of people who thrived on bartering. Now that he was home, the forest and the awful cramped living space under Rapunzel's bed felt like a dream. How was she doing, he wondered, as he deftly stole a honey cake from a market stall and bit into it, hurrying to his patron's home. She had been so very sweet, explaining how magic worked to him, but how could he have resisted the temptation to play with it? She'd know what he'd done by now – they both would.

He wished he could be a fly on the wall and watch the fallout. Maybe when he had the genie in his power he'd use a wish to spy on them. A genie granted twenty wishes, he knew that much, and he could afford to use one to keep an eye on Rapunzel for ever. It might be wise, especially until she calmed down. If the exchange was as thorough as he expected the last thing he wanted was her cursing him.

Somewhere out on the crystal water, a boat horn blared and the ships waiting to dock all jostled for space under the bright sun. He looked forward to seeing which new dignitaries and wealthy visiting nobles might disembark. What treasure there was to have here. Oh, how he'd missed all this freedom.

Freedom was what he'd given Rapunzel, though she probably wouldn't quite see it at first. Freedom from all that beauty. All that naïve trust in romance and love and *goodness*. Wanting to throw her whole life away on some idiot simply because he was handsome. Well, that wouldn't be happening anymore. He doubted she was any young nobleman's type now.

He'd given her power too. Magic in her bones. He remembered how the glimmer spindle had glowed white hot when he'd liberally sprinkled the witch's blood on it – *no good can come from three drops, but how about ten?* – that he'd thought it might burst into flames and take the tower down completely. But it had settled and Rapunzel had happily gone along with his plan and now she and the witch had changed places for good. Still, she might not thank him if they were face to face. He was glad to be out of her way for now. He'd go back when the dust had settled, and perhaps they could work together again. Her magic and his genie. The world would be theirs.

Or, he thought as he mentally reviewed their time together, maybe not.

The jetty creaked under his feet as he headed out over the water to the floating palace and the prize waiting inside. He'd get bored of her company soon enough and he didn't really want to kill her but he knew himself well enough to know he probably would. And why would he share the genie? His future was looking golden. No, he'd leave Rapunzel to figure her own future out.

'My Master,' Aladdin said with a deep bow once he was inside the delicious coolness of the opulent palace. The Great Magician had been waiting for him in his study, dressed in a fine pale blue kimono that had drops of grease on it from the fondue he was busy consuming. With a small sharp fruit knife he cut a slice off a fresh fig and pushed it into his mouth with bread and melted cheese, his lips smacking together gleefully as he ate.

'So, you have returned. And did you bring what

you promised?' He chewed while he spoke – a habit Aladdin found abhorrent – and leaned forward, eyes as greedy as his stomach. 'I've got customers waiting.'

'I have. Stolen from the witch herself.' He opened his sack up and showed his patron the collection of spindles within. 'I can tell you exactly what curse each provides.'

'Wonderful,' the Great Magician said, getting to his feet and coming closer, the fruit paring knife still in hand. 'You have redeemed yourself for the mess you made on the boat. You have your pardon and I shall give you two gold coins, how about that?'

'Whatever you wish, Master.' Aladdin saw the Great Magician's eyes narrow slightly, not used to such obsequiousness from the boy, and added, 'although I'd say four gold coins was a fairer price.'

'You'll take what you're given. Given the number of times I've saved you from the gallows and the dungeons, you're lucky I'm paying you at all.' He came forward, letting out a small belch that stank of stale cheese and old wine and worse. 'And you'd better not be holding anything back. I know you, Aladdin. You're a trickster.'

'And that's why you employ me.' The boy grinned, cocky, and the Great Magician couldn't help but smile too.

'There is truth in that. There is nothing ordinary about you, that is for sure.' He came up close to the open sack, put the small knife down on an onyx decorative table, and crouched, with more flexibility than a man of his size should have, peering into the sack, the key on the chain around his neck dangling free. 'Wonderful. And what do they each do?'

He would never hear the answer to his question and most certainly would never have need of it. Aladdin's movements were a blur of speed. Within a moment of grabbing the paring knife, he had wrapped himself around the Great Magician's back, his slim legs corset-tight around the man's waist. As they fell backwards, he began stabbing the fruit knife into his neck. The Great Magician – not so great now – had no time to scream or cry out for help. The closest he got was a wheeze of air as the knife thrust over and over into his artery, showering them both, and the room, in crimson red.

When it was done, Aladdin wriggled out from under the dead body, wiped his face clean with the magician's perfect linen napkin, and then pulled the chain and key free from the dead man's mutilated neck. He had no time to waste. The magician's guards and servants rarely interrupted one of their meetings but they would check on their master soon enough.

Not that Aladdin wanted to linger himself. Not usually one for emotions, this level of excitement was rare for him, but his whole body fizzed with the proximity of his dreams all coming true. Soon he would have a genie of his own.

He quickly unlocked the cabinet and took out the small bronze lamp, slightly battered and tarnished, the sort that would sell for pennies in an old flea market if it sold at all, and chuckled with delight. He took a deep breath and rubbed the side of the lamp hard.

At first, nothing happened, and then, as he sat the lamp down and stepped back, there was a sudden breeze, as if a wind was coming from the spout. It grew stronger, whipping loudly around him, until Aladdin had to squeeze his eyes shut and hold onto the heavy chair to keep his balance, and just as he thought he might be lifted from his feet by it, the wind dropped as swiftly as it had arrived.

'You summoned me, my new Master.'

The voice was as resonant as he remembered, echoing around the room, deep as a water witch lake and rich as thick chocolate cake from the finest bakers in the Eastern Seas. Aladdin opened his eyes and smiled. The genie wore the same red silk waistcoat and trousers over his thick, tanned body that he'd seen before, and, as he folded his forearms, his biceps bulged. He was built like one of the hardiest warriors to ever take to the Battle Lands, his green eyes like emeralds and his long black hair shining.

'I did.' Aladdin was tiny next to this giant of a man, but he didn't feel intimidated. He had learned long ago that brains could nearly always defeat brawn, and anyway, as the genie had said, he was the new master.

'I am the genie of the lamp and first I must tell you that all magic is a gift and must be treated wisely. Secondly, I ask of you what I have asked of all my masters. Do you wish to set me free or do you wish for twenty wishes?'

Aladdin dipped a hunk of bread into the melted cheese, chewed and swallowed it, before smiling at the genie.

'You look very well suited to the genie life, so I shall take the wishes.'

'And what is your first wish?' The genie bowed low, and Aladdin liked it. More people should bow to him, and they would.

'I wish this palace, its wealth, and all who serve in it, to be mine and recognised as such by the whole city.' That was a good enough place as any to start, and it would tickle him knowing how much the Great Magician would hate it.

'Is this your first wish, master?'

'It is. Make it so.' It was only after he'd spoken the words that Aladdin saw the smile twitching at the sides of the genie's mouth. Aladdin knew that smile. It was a smile of victory. What did the genie have to be victorious about?

'As you wish, Master.' The smile broke into a grin and Aladdin's eyes widened. What had he done? What had he missed?

'No, *wait*—'

But it was too late. The air hummed as if a great storm was about to break, and suddenly a red mist appeared at his feet, first just a few wisps and then a thick cloud spinning around him fast as a whirlpool.

'What's happening?' He looked up at the genie as the red pulled at his feet and legs and, in horror, he realised they were disappearing, becoming part of the mist as it worked up his body. 'Make it stop!' he screeched at the genie, but the large man just threw his head back and laughed so loudly that the whole room shook. Suddenly, as the mist engulfed him, he realised he finally understood human fear – and more than understood it – he was *feeling* it.

He unravelled, his body and the mist becoming one as he was pulled through the air, like a wave being sucked from the shore. The stench of tarnished metal filled him up as darkness enveloped him and all he could hear was the genie's laugh.

Finally, everything stilled, and he was himself again, but he was no longer in the Great Magician's palace.

It was as if he was in a cave, the ceiling barely higher than he was tall, and with maybe only eight feet of distance in any direction. He looked around the tiny space. A solitary candle burned in a sconce on the wall and there was a scattering of sand under his feet, but that was it. There was a hole in the wall at the other end and, as he peered upwards at where it narrowed to a small opening, letting some natural light in, he understood.

The lamp. He was *inside* the lamp.

Suddenly an eye appeared, huge in the gap. 'Thank you for setting me free.' The voice was so loud that the whole lamp shook, and then Aladdin's stomach dropped unpleasantly as the lamp was lifted up from the table.

'Let me out!' he screamed. 'I am your master! I wish you to release me from this trickery!'

'I have been slave to the lamp for nearly a hundred years,' the genie said. 'And now it is your turn. You should have asked me the rules of the lamp, Aladdin. But you were too keen for riches. Magic does not reward murder. If you had chosen to free me, all would have been well, but as soon as you made your first wish, you doomed yourself. *You* became the genie and *I* am now free.'

It was only then that he remembered the words he'd first heard the genie say, back before his adventure in the tower.

'But remember, Master, to try to profit from murder with magic can be a trap.'

He had paid it no heed at the time, his mind elsewhere, but now those words were lead cuffs on him. He had murdered the magician for profit and now he had imprisoned himself. Why hadn't he kept the book on genies he'd seen in the witch Gretel's library? Why had he tossed it to one side so carelessly? His heart racing, Aladdin climbed as far up the spout as he could reach, his tiny eye pleading with the enormous one peering down at him like a god.

'So, you could set me free,' he said, as warmly as he could muster. 'We could *both* be free. I'm just a child who's had a hard life. I was wrong to be greedy but I have learned my lesson. You can keep the palace. I will go away, join one of the boats. Earn an honest living.'

'Oh, Aladdin,' the genie laughed again. 'I know you too well. I know the things you've done. The barbaric murders. Unnecessary murders committed for your own pleasure. I think the world is a safer place with you in the lamp, and so in the lamp you will stay. And, I intend to make sure you are undisturbed by a summoning for a very long time ... At least until after my own natural death. I have no desire to be looking over my shoulder for your spiteful revenge.'

Aladdin kicked at the metal walls of his tiny prison until his toes bled, then the world went dark as the genie dropped the lamp into the sack with the spindles and carried him out of the palace he would never own.

'I will kill you!' he screamed, but no one answered.

No one would answer for a very, very long time.

Twenty-Seven

Rapunzel could not calm down, her rage at the injustice of her fate burning her up from the inside. All she had wanted was to love and be loved, and, yet, time after time she'd been abandoned and deceived. First her father, leaving her with a witch and promising to return, then the young king whose only passion for her was physical, and then – the worst of them all – Aladdin. Her best friend. Her *only* friend. How could he have done this to her? Turned her into a bitter old witch. He hadn't broken her heart, but he'd stolen her *life*. He had let her believe that he was helping her and for what? So he could steal Aunt Gretel's spindles?

'Everyone has betrayed me,' she hissed, storming around her room on aching legs, red sparks itching the tips of her fingers. 'How can I live like this?'

'Shhh, shhh, you must calm down.' Gretel tried to put her arms around her, to soothe her, but Rapunzel couldn't bear it and pushed her away. Seeing her own beauty looking back at her, firm, soft skin and her thick, golden hair tucked away in the braids, knowing it was all lost? Aunt Gretel had her beauty now *and* her youth. How could she face that?

'The young king was a fool, I see that now, I would never have loved him for long, though my intentions were honest. But Aladdin made a fool of me. He must be *laughing* at me. What did I do to deserve this? Nothing!' She paused as a clay jug smashed.

'You really have to be still.' Gretel held her shoulders. 'Magic and uncontrolled emotion are a dangerous mix. Until you've learned how to—'

'I don't want your magic!' Rapunzel snapped. 'I want my beauty back!'

Gretel pulled her in close and this time she didn't fight it. 'I know. I wish I could change it but I can't. We have to find our way through this. We can still be happy. We can—'

'Nobody will ever love me now. My own father never came back for me! What does that say about me?'

Gretel sat her down on the bed, holding both her hands tightly. 'You are kind and sweet and think the best of people, and those are excellent qualities. I was wrong to hold all men accountable for those who had tried to hurt me in my own youth. Aladdin's trick is not your fault, and I wonder if in some twisted way, based on the note he left, he thought he was doing something nice for you.'

'Something *nice*? How could this be nice?'

***

Gretel could see Rapunzel in her own lilac-flecked eyes. The hurt. The upset. The lost innocence of it all.

'There are some people in the world who are built wrong,' she said. 'Perhaps Aladdin was one of those.'

When Rapunzel had been in the kitchen, refusing to let her in, and eating cake while she raged, Gretel had heard a commotion coming from the forest. Cries of discovery. Slaughtered soldiers in a pit. She couldn't imagine the young king would have committed such an act, so that only left one likely candidate. This vanished friend of Rapunzel's. If he was as monstrous as that, then they were both lucky to be alive, but this was no time to try to explain that to Rapunzel.

'As for the young king – well, youth makes mistakes and there is no harm in that. And then there is your father.' She took a deep breath and knew that although it would make Rapunzel hate her, she had to finally tell the truth. 'He didn't abandon you. Not really. He believed he would be coming back.'

'What do you mean?' Rapunzel stiffened and, as butterflies nibbled at Gretel's insides, she knew there was no going back now. The truth must come out.

'He came for a spindle to save a kingdom. But he didn't know that he and the kingdom would be lost for a hundred years the moment the curse was activated. He didn't come back, not because he didn't love you, but because he couldn't.'

'You did this.' Rapunzel's eyes widened. 'You did all of this. You *stole* me.'

'I'm sorry,' Gretel said, tears pricking her eyes. 'It was a terrible thing to do. I was so lonely. I didn't think. I—'

'You *did* think.' Rapunzel was on her feet and her eyes blazed with hatred. 'But only of yourself. You even took my memories of him. Of everything I had before. Who I was. You let me hate him because it suited you!'

The pain hit Gretel hard, her own and the wave of emotion that radiated from Rapunzel, but although she knew there was no coming back from it, she also knew she would rather the girl hated her than her own father. Perhaps this was love after all. 'You're right. I did.' She held back her own tears. This was no time for self-pity. She'd brought it all on herself. 'And if I could take it back I would. If I could change this curse upon us I would. I love you as if you were my own, and I hate myself for what I have done. I wanted to save you from the world of men, and instead I've caused all this damage. When I was young—'

'I don't care about when you were young!' Rapunzel's words made the tower shake, and she was happy to see Gretel flinch and cover her ears. Rapunzel couldn't believe what she was hearing. Everything – her whole life in this tower – was built on Gretel's lies. 'It's all your fault!'

'Please, Rapunzel, stop . . .'

But she wouldn't stop. She couldn't. Her anger was a storm inside her, a black tempest that threatened to consume her entirely. Gretel and Aladdin had done this. If Gretel hadn't imprisoned her with lies and magic, then Aladdin would never have been able to trick her into the curse. She hated them both, but Gretel most of all. Gretel was here in front of her and she would make her pay.

'I never want to see you again,' she said quietly. 'I

hate you. I will hate you for ever for what you've done to me. You can live in this tower alone for the rest of your days for all I care.' She laughed bitterly. 'In fact, you can live here until true love saves you, and if such a day should come to pass then the tower will fall into ruin, so no one can ever cause such heartache here again. I make that my first curse.'

She turned and stormed out of the room and down the stairs, not wanting Gretel to see the tears that came as readily as the red sparks building around her, her ice-white hair dancing with them. She flicked a finger and the door opened for the last time, and she left the tower for ever. She walked out across the flower and herb garden and they wilted under her gaze as the sky grew dark.

When she reached the copse of trees, so close to where the young king had sat to woo a stupid girl in the window, she turned to look back. Gretel was at the window looking back at her. 'I'm sorry,' she called. 'I'm so sorry. *I love you, Rapunzel.*'

Rapunzel clicked her fingers and red lightning – not the blue she expected, the blue of natural magic – shot from their tips to the sky and back again, and she knew, as if she'd always had so much magic in her, that the curse was sealed. Gretel was trapped in the tower and would stay there for ever.

MAGIC

Only true love could break the curse and, as she had learned at her own bitter cost, true love was rarer than magic.

Twenty-Eight

The storm lasted two days, strange red lightning butting streaks across the dark sky as rain flooded the river, threatening to drown the village itself, and in the distance fire rained down over the Far Mountain, and the people were sure they heard a dragon sing.

After the horrific discovery of the murdered soldiers, followed so quickly by the unnatural storm, it took all of Conrad's geniality to stop some of his neighbours going straight to the white tower with burning torches. It was clear to all that none of this was normal, and while they might not be able to blame the witch for the brutal deaths of the mercenaries, they were sure they were somehow connected to the storm that had ruined their fields and drowned their wheat supplies. His sister and her husband also

spoke up and showed the other villagers the wonderful blanket that Gretel had given to help their baby for
no cost, and that helped turn the cries for revenge into
disgruntled rumblings.

Once the water had drained away, it turned out that
their stores were not as ruined as they first thought.
Conrad donated his gold coins to the collection and
two young men were sent to buy more grain from a
neighbouring town. The village quietened and life
returned to normal – for they were all kind and gentle
people at heart – but Conrad was still unsettled.

He had been to the white tower three times to check
on Gretel and Rapunzel but no one had answered his
calls or come down to the door to speak to him or
ask for supplies. He had gone back at night and seen
lights burning inside, in Rapunzel's room, so he knew
someone was there, but he also knew that something
was very wrong.

The storm had been magical, he knew that, even if
there was not that much call for magic this deep into
the forest, but there had been something wrong about
it. If a witch brought a storm, everyone knew the
lightning would be blue, but the lightning that frac-
tured their sky so violently was blood red. Unnatural
magic. So he trusted his gut that something was very
wrong indeed.

A full ten days after the storm, Conrad was at his wit's end, and so he brought a blanket and knapsack of food and made a small camp under the copse outside the tower. 'I'm not leaving until one of you speaks to me,' he called up. 'I just need to know you're well. And if there is anything I can fetch for you. Whatever has gone wrong, whatever brought that storm, maybe I can help you?'

There was no answer, and it took all his patience not to shout up at the window, his anxiety tipping into frustration. He was worried about Gretel. In all her years here – a hazy amount of time because he couldn't really remember a day when she *wasn't* here – nothing like this had ever happened. She'd lived quietly and peacefully alongside the villagers.

'You're being very unfair!' he said, eventually. 'It's cruel to let someone worry about you. And despite your determination to be seen as heartless, Gretel, I believe you to be otherwise!' Still, no one came to the window. 'And I thought more of you too, Rapunzel!' he added, before turning and going to his small camp by the copse. 'Very well. The grass is soft and the branches of these trees will provide me with a roof. I can stay here indefinitely. You're going to have to show your faces at some point. And I intend to be here when you do.'

Twenty-Nine

Conrad had been camped outside for two days, talking up to her about whatever took his fancy, trying to revive her plant and herb gardens, but of all of it, it was his cheerful singing at his campfire that was driving Gretel mad, and it seemed to follow her wherever she went in the tower.

She drifted, desolate, from room to room, wishing she had the strength to throw herself from the one remaining window and be done with it all. She would do too, if it didn't mean wrecking Rapunzel's body. She couldn't do that. It would feel like an added crime on top of all the damage her bitterness had already wrought.

With no magic to hold it in place, Rapunzel's long golden hair – *her* long golden hair – had started to unravel into matted lengths, tripping her up at every turn, and in the end, after she'd finished the last of the wine in a fit of self-pity, she'd grabbed a knife and hacked it off at her shoulders, kicking the vast swathe of hair into a pile in the corner of the room. She cried all over again when she saw it was now the length Rapunzel had always begged her for on those long nights of washing and brushing. She should have let the girl have her way. She should have done a lot of things. She cried some more, far more than she ever had been able to in her own body, and then nibbled on the last of the bread. She hadn't been hungry for days, but her bodice had grown tighter and she loosened the laces so she could breathe.

What would happen when the food ran out? Would she starve to death? Maybe. Or maybe not. All that would depend on the nature of Rapunzel's curse. Maybe the cupboard would automatically replenish itself. It was strange to be the one at the mercy of magic, but she couldn't deny being glad to be free of it, even if it meant she would die in this tower she'd created so long ago. Magic had never felt like a gift to her. She had wished it away so many times when she was young and finally, although not in any way she would have chosen, her wish had come true. But that was so often the way with wishes, as many who made them found out.

Conrad's song was setting her teeth on edge. It was a country song, which was probably quite joyful when sung properly, but it was clear that Conrad could not hold a tune. Every note was a flat or a sharp and all in the wrong places. It was bad enough that she felt queasy all the time, and now the noise was giving her a headache.

'Just stop, you foolish man!' she snapped, finally going to the window.

'Rapunzel!' He got to his feet and came rushing closer to the window, a beaming grin on his face. 'What a relief to see you. And Gretel? Where is your aunt?'

'It's none of your business,' she snapped at him. 'I don't want you here! Go back to your hovel and get on with your pathetic little life and leave me – us – be.' She waved him away with her hands as if shooing him. 'Go back to where you're wanted.'

His smile fell, and at first she thought it was because her words had stung him, but then she saw his expression was not one of hurt, but of confusion.

'What? What are you staring at? Get your things and leave.'

'Gretel?' he said, quietly, his head tilting sideways. 'Is that you? How can that be?'

She stared down at him, momentarily lost for words, and once again tears began to fall.

'It *is* you,' Conrad said, surer of himself this time.

'Am I me?' she asked hopefully. 'Do I look like me again? There was a curse and a boy who came with the young king and – oh, it's too long a story but everything went wrong.' Maybe the glimmer was starting to wear off. Maybe the wicked boy hadn't done as much harm as he thought. 'Am I turning back into me again?'

'You look like Rapunzel,' Conrad said. 'But I'd know you anywhere, Gretel.'

'How?' she asked, softly, her heart suddenly racing, although she didn't understand why. He could see her. He could truly *see* her despite what his eyes were telling him.

'Firstly, because Rapunzel is never so convincing with her dismissive tone as you are when you're trying your hardest to seem cold-hearted, and secondly, well secondly –' he paused and took a deep breath '– secondly, because I love you, Gretel. I think you are wonderful. Despite what the world did to you, you did no harm to anyone. You locked yourself away when you could have used your magic against us all. I don't know what has happened to bring this change about, and I don't know if you can fix it, but I will love you either way and I will help you however I can.'

'I don't have any magic anymore. When we changed and Rapunzel became me, the magic went with her. She left me locked up here because . . . Conrad, I've been so very foolish. I did a terrible thing keeping her here.' She felt a rush of emotion, and all of a sudden she wanted to feel him holding her tight, even if he couldn't make everything better. He could make *her* feel less broken and that would be a start.

'Come down, Gretel. Let me in so I can help you.'

How could she not have seen it all before? The *goodness* inside him. The way she'd always felt safe around him. Why she hadn't taken his gold for the blanket. She wondered if maybe she loved him too, a strong steady love that had grown quietly over the years, creeping up on her like an ivy so slowly that she hadn't noticed that it had consumed her. Was it true love? Was that what this feeling was? How could she be sure?

'I can't. There's no door anymore, only this window. I'm trapped here.'

'I'll get a ladder,' he said, and then she could see him calculate the distance to the window before he added, 'Or make a new one that will reach. Unless you have a rope up there?'

Dusk was falling and the nausea that had plagued her all day was finally lifting, and suddenly she realised that she *did* want to get out of the tower. She had made so many mistakes, but the glimmer wasn't her fault. Aladdin wasn't her fault. And how could she put anything right with Rapunzel if she died up here?

'Yes, the one from the pulley. Wait there.' Her heart leapt at the thought of her imminent freedom and she ran out to the hall and pulled the long rope through Rapunzel's bedroom and threw it out of the window. It didn't quite reach the ground but was only a few feet short. It was perfect. She started to climb out of the window but Conrad stopped her.

'Let me test it first. Just in case.'

'It will be fine.'

'It may well be, but better to be safe than sorry.' He jumped, grabbing the rope and planting his feet on the wall to help his climb. He'd made it about three feet up when Gretel heard strands of the rope starting to snap.

'Stop!' she called down, urgently. 'It's breaking!'

He'd just got himself vertical again when the rope broke and he dropped to the grass with a thud.

'Are you all right?' Gretel's heart was in her mouth.

'Are you hurt?' She couldn't bear it if anything bad happened to Conrad because of her. She couldn't bear if anything happened to him full stop.

'Only my pride,' he called up cheerfully. 'I have plenty of padding. And don't worry. I'll make a ladder. Even if it takes a week or so we'll get you down.'

A week suddenly seemed like a very long time. What if the food and water didn't replenish itself? She looked around the workshop, and then her heart lifted. 'I've got an idea.'

Thirty

She might not have magic in her bones anymore but she knew which of the spinning wheels did what, and once she'd found the one she was looking for, left behind by Aladdin, Gretel carried it down to the workshop and then added a touch of oil to the heavy matted coils of her cut hair and brushed out the knots. She found herself humming as she worked, her heart a hundred times lighter. Conrad was waiting for her outside the tower. There was a life waiting for her – if she was brave enough to claim it.

As dusk turned to night, the candles on the walls lit themselves and burned in their sconces, and the moon washed the room with extra light, creating a spotlight on Gretel, concentrating as she started to spin. As the wheel turned the magic within came alive, spinning the hair to gold, which she then plaited into a rope. It would be strong. It would hold her. It had to.

By the time the first birds were calling out to greet the day, Gretel's hands were sore and her back ached almost as much as it had in her original body, but she stood up and stretched, satisfied with her work.

At the window, she looked down to see Conrad smiling back up at her as she threw the thick gold coil out through the window, watching it unfurl all the way to the floor. 'I've attached it to the pulley frame,' she said. 'And it should hold.' It was tied to the metal in several knots and she was sure that if she climbed down fast it wouldn't come free before she reached the grass. Hopefully the knots would get tighter and more secure with her weight. There was only one way to find out.

'Be careful,' Conrad said, frowning with worry. 'Are you sure I shouldn't come up?'

She looked at him, exasperated. 'Then we'd both have to climb down again.'

Her heart in her mouth, suddenly very aware of how high the tower really was, she seized the golden rope and, without looking down, carefully climbed out of the window, gripping her thighs tight, finding purchase in the plaited metal.

Inch by inch, Conrad calling out encouragement from below, she slowly lowered herself down. Her shoulders and legs screamed with the tension, but the grass got closer and when she finally dared to look, she was well over halfway. She allowed herself a small laugh at the proximity of her freedom.

'That's it! Keep going!'

Her eyes met Conrad's and she could see how proud he was, but just as she grinned at him, realising there was only a short way left to go, something changed. Despite her slow movement down, the rope was starting a slow movement *upwards.*

'What's happening?' Conrad's smile fell as he saw what she was feeling. She was going in the wrong direction.

She looked up to see the rope was being pulled back up through the window, and taking her with it. 'It's the curse!' she called down, frantic. 'The pulley must be turning to bring me back into the tower!'

She had been maybe eight feet from the ground. Now she was ten and rising. She looked down and then up again. The rope was moving faster.

'What shall I do?' she cried in despair. 'What shall I *do*?'

'Let go!' Conrad stood beneath her on the grass, his arms open. 'Let go and I'll catch you.'

'You can't.' He was too far below. He'd never manage it. Her back would break. 'You'll miss.'

'I won't.' He smiled confidently at her. 'I promise I'll catch you. Now let go, Gretel. Trust me.'

Looking down, Gretel felt a sudden sense of calm. She *did* trust him. She trusted him with her life.

She closed her eyes and did as she was told.

She let go.

***

They didn't tell the villagers about the glimmer or her true identity, but instead said simply that the witch had set Rapunzel free and gone to live elsewhere in the woods. Both were quietly pleased that there was some genuine sadness that she had left and Gretel realised that perhaps they had not feared her in the way she thought all people did. But she was also glad to no longer have the word *witch* hanging over her. Conrad understood her concern that the villagers might think she stole Rapunzel's youth intentionally and if there were ever any natural disasters she might always be considered the culprit. It was human nature to look for someone to blame in bad times. It was easier for her to become

Rapunzel, and while sometimes, at night, when it was just the two of them in their bed, he would whisper her real name, even he called her Rapunzel in public.

The cause of the nausea quickly became clear – Conrad pointing out the obvious – that perhaps she was with child, and as she bloomed, so did their love. No one questioned how the young, beautiful girl from the tower had fallen in love with the bow-legged, older man, because as they grew to know her, they all felt that Rapunzel was somewhat older than her years and all could see how well suited she and Conrad were and how happy they were together.

They married at the end of the first summer, and the whole village came out to celebrate with them. The baby girl, the young king's daughter in flesh, but Conrad's in heart, arrived the next spring, and their happiness was complete.

Or almost complete.

Gretel still had a corner of sadness in her heart that not even Conrad or her daughter's love could dispel. She missed Rapunzel and worried about her, and often, at night, when she tossed and turned, the tiny baby in the crib beside them, Conrad knew Gretel was dreaming of the girl she had become. He would tell her he was going out to check the rabbit traps further in the forest, but he would spend days looking for Rapunzel to no avail.

He had a feeling she didn't want to be found.

Epilogue

At first she was all hate and rage, a whirlwind of unnatural red magic, a body and soul that should never have been joined, and the forest animals, from the highest butterfly to the tiniest beetle, fled at her approach. She breathed bitterness on summer blooms, and walked until her feet were blistered in her boots, and then she walked some more. She walked until she was exhausted, and only then, when she finally crumpled to the mossy ground in a surprise clearing in the thickest part of the forest, did her anger fade enough to allow her to sleep.

She slept for two days straight and when she awoke, she saw the forest had been busy.

The animals, recognising a wild creature like

themselves, had brought berries and twigs and leaves and other things that were of value to them and left them around her as gifts, and when she saw them, she cried for the first time since leaving the tower. She cried for herself, she cried for her lost life, she cried for things she did not truly understand.

Once she was done crying, she realised that the clearing reminded her a little of where the white tower stood, and there was a stream and flowers, but the forest was tight around it and she had a feeling it would only let people find her when she allowed it. She was still filled with hate, but she distilled it down to Aladdin, for he was the one who had brought this fate upon her, and she wondered if he would be curious enough to seek her out again. She would be ready for him, if he did.

As she calmed, she found that she was starving, and so her magic built her a cottage.

It made the walls of cake and the filler of icing and the window frames of strawberry liquorice – every part of it was edible. It seemed, she thought, as she broke off a piece of marzipan doorframe that immediately re-built itself, that she had gained Gretel's sweet tooth along with her magic.

Inside, the cottage was cosy, and at the heart of it was a large oven. Big enough to bake as much bread and as many cakes as she wanted. Big enough for a child to climb into, she thought, as she stared at it and once again remembered Aladdin's smile.

She tried not to think about Gretel, but her dreams were not under her control and she would wake, sweating, with tears on her pillow, and found herself regretting her curse. She could not forgive her aunt fully, but she could go some way in understanding her. She missed Gretel, now more than ever, as she finally figured out what the daytime nausea she'd been feeling since leaving the tower meant.

She waited a full year, and then, after sending a raven to see what she suspected might be true, she strapped her own infant daughter to her back, locked up her cottage, leaving it in the protection of the forest, and journeyed back the way she'd come in such a cowl of rage.

It was easy to find the route she had forged in her rage. She had adjusted to the weight of the magic in her bones so that she barely noticed it now, and her stride was strong. The ground was still recovering, the moss drier than in the surrounding areas, and she followed the almost invisible path all the way back to the village that had once been all she knew. She paused as she passed the crumbling tower, and the door opened to her. She took what she wanted from the collection of books and then left it to continue its rot.

She watched Conrad's cottage from beyond the treeline for two whole days.

It was strange, seeing herself. Humming and scrubbing sheets and shirts in the stream. Bringing Conrad a cool drink while he chopped wood. Rocking a baby in her arms in the afternoon sunshine. She listened to the laughter that came from the cottage and it made her smile. She could forgive Gretel after all.

While they slept, she crept out and left what she'd brought on the wooden step, and then retreated to the woods to nurse her own child and sleep under the canopy of trees, where not so very long ago, Aladdin had made his camp.

In the morning she waited until they woke, and not long after sunrise, as smoke started out of the small chimney, the door opened and Conrad came out, yawning. He froze when he saw what was waiting on the step, then called for his wife.

'Rapunzel, look.' It was strange to hear her own name calling someone else and she decided that maybe that was what she should do to call herself

Gretel and be done with the past – and, after a moment, she watched herself emerge, baby at her bosom, and gasp.

The rainbow blanket was folded carefully, glittering with magic in the dappling sunlight. On top she had placed a perfect pink peony, picked that morning from near the ruined tower. She watched as her aunt burst into tears and crouched, staring at the baby blanket as if perhaps it was an illusion.

'It's from her,' she said, and her tears came harder. 'She's all right. I think she's all right. Oh, Conrad, that is more of a gift than I could have hoped for. She's going to be all right.'

She unfolded the soft wool and prepared to put the baby in it when Conrad stopped her. 'What if it's not a charm?' he asked, worried. 'What if it's a curse?'

In her place in the woods, she held her breath, and then felt tears of her own blurring her vision as her aunt smiled. 'I trust her, Conrad,' the young woman said softly, as she swaddled their gurgling child in the blanket. 'I trust her because I love her.'

She picked up the baby, and glanced towards the woods, scanning hopefully but in vain for a glimpse of the child she had loved first, and then leaned her head on Conrad's shoulder as he wrapped one arm around her.

Satisfied, Gretel the witch turned and started her long walk back to her candy cottage – and her own future.

She did not look back.

Credits

Sarah Pinborough and Gollancz would like to thank everyone at Orion who worked on the publication of *Magic*.

Agent
Veronique Baxter

Editorial
Gillian Redfearn
Bethan Morgan
Zakirah Alam

Copy-editor
Tara Loder

Proofreader
Margaret Gray

Editorial Management
Jane Hughes
Charlie Panayiotou
Lucy Bilton
Samantha Jepp Panteli

Audio
Paul Stark
Louise Richardson
Georgina Cutler

Contracts
Dan Herron
Ellie Bowker
Oliver Chacón

Design
Nick Shah
Rachel Lancaster
Deborah Francois
Helen Ewing

Finance
Nick Gibson
Jasdip Nandra
Sue Baker
Tom Costello

Inventory
Jo Jacobs
Dan Stevens

Marketing
Lucy Cameron

Production
Paul Hussey
Katie Horrocks

Publicity
Jenna Petts

Sales
Catherine Worsley
Victoria Laws
Esther Waters
Tolu Ayo-Ajala
Karin Burnik
Anne-Katrine Buch
Frances Doyle
Group Sales teams across
Digital, Field, Interna-
tional and Non-Trade

Operations
Group Sales Operations
team

Rights
Rebecca Folland
Tara Hiatt
Ben Fowler
Alice Cottrell
Ruth Blakemore
Marie Henckel